A CARSON & LANEY NOVEL

DEEPER WATER

ONCE AND FOREVER BOOK 3

LAUREN STEWART

ALSO BY LAUREN STEWART

The Hyde series

Hyde, an urban fantasy

Jekyll

Strange Case

The Heights

Unseen

Unearthed

Into the Light

Once and Forever

Darker Water

Virtually Impossible

Deeper Water

No Experience Required

Second Bite

Stick around to find out how to sign up for Lauren's mailing list and get exclusive extras from the *Once and Forever* series.

For my dad.

I was waiting until I wrote a book I'd actually let you read before dedicating one to you.

I waited too long.

I miss you every day.

Carson and Laney's
After Happily-Ever-After

≈

Once Upon a Time...

...there was a frog who, with great care, held the heart of the most beautiful woman in his entire world. On occasion, he wondered if she were daft or simply not as smart as she looked. For truly, why would a beauty so rare ever desire someone like him, unless she was slightly, mostly, or entirely insane? Odder still was when the woman spoke of seeing him transform, become who he was meant to be, become someone worthy of her beauty. This, the frog found impossible to believe. For he would never deserve her love. Nor could he see the transformation she claimed to see. For he could no longer remember who he was before the woman came into his life, before he'd known the joy, contentment, and pride of being with her.

And so, though he could not believe it, he could believe her. *He took the woman at her word, knowing her to always be true. After all, they had saved each other from secrets that had nearly drowned them both. So neither would ever allow that curse to darken their lives again.*

Unfortunately, as it happens in most, if not all, stories with happy endings, our frog and his woman had a lesson yet to learn:

Life's turbulent water does not simply calm and go silent for even the truest of loves. And sometimes, two lovers are wrapped too tightly in each other's warmth to see the crashing wave...until it is too late.

1

CARSON

ALL THIS OVER A FUCKING ROCK.

A fucking rock tucked into the pocket of my jeans that would combust and set my pants on fire any second now. A fitting end, considering all the lies I'd told to keep it secret.

My curvy little Lane would forgive me, though. She'd forgiven way stupider shit. Example number one: The whole friends-with-benefits I'd honestly believed would work. It's hysterical now, looking back on it. I'd actually thought I could take her body without wanting her mind, her wit, her patience, and the rest of her...forever.

Examples number two...and three...on up to about thirty, were the far less pleasant issues with my family. My seriously fucked-up childhood, my *still* seriously fucked-up mother and stepsister, and, of course, me. A true mess of a man who, due to recent developments, was becoming messier and messier.

So yeah, she'd forgive me...*if* I ever gathered up enough courage to tell the most amazing woman I'd ever known why I'd been such an inexcusable dumbass lately.

Yep, my current sense of self could be described by America's favorite seven-letter word. If I remembered correctly, only two other people had ever called me a dumbass. A few minutes later, both of them had taken it back. Well, they would've, if my fist hadn't screwed up full use of their jaws.

But that shit was back in the bad old days, before Lane had domesticated me and transformed me into a decent person. Except for every day over the last month, in which I would've had to agree with those two dickheads. At least while I anxiously searched for the "perfect" rock. And when I had to decide which metal would keep the "perfect" rock from falling off Lane's finger. Because, obviously, it had to be the "perfect" metal with exactly the "perfect" amount of swirly shit around it for my perfect woman—no air quotes around that one 'cause it's a fact.

Then the impressively manipulative jeweler had done the whole "The stone is stunning, *but* it would look even better with a few slightly smaller diamonds around it. For balance." For balance. Right. God forbid I give Lane an unbalanced stone. It might remind her of the unbalanced man who'd given it to her. Although, for all I knew, diamonds were happier traveling in packs.

I'm not stupid. Well, I'm not *that* stupid. I didn't care about the money—Lane was worth double everything in the store combined—but *she* was the only one allowed to screw me now.

Unfortunately, the salesman knew how to play to his audience. In my anxiety-induced word vomit, I may have mentioned that Lane was an incredible artist—not with metal and rocks though. Lane was a genius with wood—the only wood I'd ever wrapped my hands around, along with the kind that came from trees. So when the guy wondered aloud if I might prefer to have a simple custom design created by some guy in New York City who was a "true artist," I caved.

In the spirit of being the biggest dumbass in the jewelry store, I think I said yes to everything. I *definitely* said yes to the artist in New York City, because opting for a custom design that had to be shipped across the country a couple times meant I could put off the big question for a few more weeks.

Plus, if the "true artist" in New York was anything like the artist he was making the piece for, he'd be obsessively working on it for *way* longer than any normal human being would have patience for. Gotta love those artists with their freakish perfectionism. They made the rest of us feel sane in comparison.

However, the same couldn't be said for whoever had made up the rules of engagement. They all deserved to be shot. No one should be able to turn a grown man into a pathetic twit. And no one should force a guy into fucking *weeks* of shopping for anything other than adult toys and lingerie.

Don't even get me started on every sap who's ever posted a YouTube video of their proposal. It's just not fair. After finally finding a rock, I was supposed to come up with a YouTube-acceptable way to ask her? Way too much pressure. Which was exactly why I'd put it off for so long. My brother had already done it *twice*—once when he knew it was a terrible idea before they'd even cut the wedding cake. The second time was, without a doubt, the best and smartest thing he'd ever done, other than having me as a brother.

That sweeter, smarter, longer-lasting wedding cake was going to be served in a few days on a French Polynesian island, which made it all the more important I get this proposal shit with Lane done *now*. Before everyone at Hayden and Andi's wedding got a chance to ask us fourteen billion *more* times when it was our turn.

My last excuse collapsed when I'd hung up with the jeweler this morning after hearing the words, "Mr. Bennett, the ring arrived and—"

Said ring had been burning a hole in my pants ever since. A chunk of very expensive coal in a tiny box I couldn't stop touching. In fact, my hand was shoved so deeply in my pocket, petting that damn velvet to check if it was still there, everyone I passed probably thought I was just another pervert playing with his cock. Gotta love San Francisco—*nothing* surprised people here.

When Lane had called to ask if I would meet her at our café so we could talk after work, I felt terrible. What if she was so annoyed with me that "talk" meant break up? It would serve me right for being such a dumbass. I'm not even sure I could call myself a man anymore. I'd been completely emasculated by one simple question. Granted, the answer to that question would pretty much set up everything else for the rest of my days, but it wasn't going to cause my life to end. Right?

It wasn't, was it?

Dumb. Ass.

No matter how hard I tried to hide my lies and dumbass-like reflexes, Lane had definitely noticed. Last night, I think I hurt her feelings when I yelled, "Are you fucking kidding me?" and threw the remote at the TV. I couldn't explain my frustration to her, so all she saw was her boyfriend freaking out over a commercial. But, in my defense, what was I supposed to do? It had been a *jewelry* commercial. Now I knew why the guys looked so damn happy in them, though—they'd made it through the process without killing someone.

So, here we were: Lane looking as beautiful as always, and me, trying like hell not to look like I was jerking off while fully clothed.

Fuck it. I needed to get this over with before I made her hate me. I couldn't handle this shit any longer. Thankfully, I stopped myself from shoving the box at her while we were in line to place our coffee order. A proposal had to be special, something memorable, something clickable on YouTube.

"I missed a spot," she said, staring at her fingers.

"Huh?"

She held out her palm. "My glove tore while I was finishing a table this morning. When the varnish dries under my nails, it's annoying as hell."

"No glove, no love, babe."

She showed me her nails. Well, actually, she showed me just one nail...on one finger...right in the middle.

"Exactly what I was thinking," I said, winking. "I even have an extra *glove* in my wallet, so..." I had to laugh at her expression —sexy frustration. Thankfully I didn't say that out loud. It sounded way too much like "sexual frustration," an expression I prayed I'd never have reason to say out loud.

"Come on, babe. You know I love it when you're dirty. Just not *that* kind of dirty. Go wash up. I'll grab the drinks."

"Thanks." She raised up onto her toes and kissed me quickly before heading toward the bathrooms.

While she was gone, I picked up our coffees and took them to our spot in the back of the café. It was where we'd first met, where we'd second met, where we'd gotten to know each other. Where I'd briefly forgotten how much I wanted to fuck her and had actually started caring about who she was. Which meant, in a way, it was where I'd fallen in love with her too.

Lots of good memories in this spot. Huh. Maybe this was the perfect place after all. Sentimental, spontaneous, filled with people who were in too much of a rush to gawk. Perfect.

With frequent glances to make sure she wasn't coming back yet, I slipped the box from my pocket and stared at the ring for as long as I dared. The artist in New York was worth every penny, maybe even worth all the agony I'd gone through.

Even *I* had to admit the rock looked gorgeous—big but not grotesquely big, nothing Lane would be embarrassed by. The designer had also come up with another setting the ring could slip into so Lane could wear it as a necklace while she worked. I left that part in the box and looked around for romantic inspiration.

How should I do it? Lane wasn't crazy about surprises, but surprises made good stories, sometimes even YouTube-acceptable stories. I slipped the ring under her coffee, then centered it so the cup didn't look like the Leaning Tower of Java. When she lifted it up, she'd see the bling, be surprised, and this hell would be over. Hallelujah.

As soon as I saw her coming back from the bathroom, I leaned back in my chair and tried to act normal.

"All clean now." She flopped into her chair, setting her bag down next to her. "You can dirty me up later."

"Promise?" My smile was plastered on, all my nerves and attention focused on what to say when she picked up the cup.

"Yes, but you'll have to be patient. After this, I should go back to work for a while. The opening of the new lobby is coming up so fast, and I still have to finish the last table before we leave tomorrow."

The only reason Lane hadn't figured out what I'd been obsessing over for the last few weeks was because she'd been obsessing over her art installation for *months*. The owner of a building downtown had commissioned her to build a series of reclaimed wood tables for his new lobby. It was a huge deal with a huge paycheck and a great opportunity to showcase her art. I hadn't been allowed to see it yet, but I took full credit for all her hard work. After all, supposedly *I* was her inspiration.

Shit, what if the tables were all shaped like dumbasses? Nah, she'd started the project before I turned into one. Phew.

"Then," she continued, "while we're at Hayden's wedding..." She still hadn't touched her coffee cup. What was she waiting for? "...the finish will be able to cure"—*something, something. I wasn't really listening*—"Once we get back"—*something about movers*—"over to the building and set them up. It should only take a day or so..."

"Uh-huh." I hoped she wasn't saying anything vital because, at some point, I'd forgotten how to understand English.

"...the positioning is perfect, but it's hard not to worry."

"Worry, yeah," I mumbled. "Gotcha." I tried to keep my eyes off the damn cup, tried to pay attention to what she was saying, but honestly, I couldn't hear her over all the panic in my head. Why hadn't she lifted the fucking thing yet?

"...I'm going to pay the movers with my body," she said. "A hot quickie with each of them, you know?"

"Sure, makes sense," I said, nodding like good boyfriends do.

"I need some advice though. Should I tag team them or try doing a double or even triple penetra—?"

"You gonna drink that?" I pointed at her cup—a grande cream-and-sugar with a single shot of decaf espresso floating on top. Her favorite. No idea why she called it coffee.

She looked at me with a raised eyebrow, probably because I'd just cut her off mid-sentence, although it could've been a bunch of other reasons, too. But I had way bigger things to worry about. And possibly regret.

I sighed. "Never mind." This was the worst idea I'd ever had. The best idea now was to figure out a way to get out of it. "It's probably cold by now."

I reached for the cup with both hands, one of them sliding along the table so I could scoop the ring up without her seeing it. "I'll get you another one."

She grabbed the cup, not letting me have it.

"Is it let's-ignore-Laney-day today?" she asked, her forehead all squished up. "Why are you the first and only one celebrating it?"

"I just—" This really couldn't have been going any better.

King of poetry and romance right here, especially because I couldn't form an actual sentence.

Thankfully, she was distracted when someone called her name. Followed by a squeal that, also thankfully, no one but her ex-roommate Hillary could manage.

"Guess who's getting married!"

2

CARSON

LANE SHRIEKED. I cringed. How in the hell had Hillary found out? *I'd* barely had time to come to grips with it. And Lane hadn't actually agreed to it yet.

"It was *soooo* romantic, Laney!" Hillary ran over to us. "I cried when he asked. Honestly, sobbing, ugly crying!"

Wait. *She'd* cried. When *he'd* asked. "Eric asked you to marry him?"

She stopped her happy dance to look at me in silence for half a second. "No, Carson. I'm talking about Prince Harry. Yep, it's true. He dumped Meghan, and now we're engaged."

I had no idea who the hell she was talking about, but Hillary's dramatic sigh conveyed the message.

"Uh...right," I said intelligently. "Guess my brain shut off for a second. Because...I'm so excited for you."

They both seemed to accept my excuse, so maybe my luck was turning. If I could just grab the cup and what was under it without either of them seeing anything, I'd consider it a good day. Not the colossal failure it would be if Lane found out how unromantic I was. A ring shoved under a coffee cup wouldn't make her ugly cry, unless it was from disappointment.

Hillary half-sat on the arm of Lane's chair. "I was just sitting there, regular boring day at work, when in walks this line of delivery guys with more flowers than you've ever seen. Seriously, Eric must have bought out the entire flower shop."

"Were you freaking out?" Lane asked.

"A little, but I think I was in shock." Hillary looked so happy I almost forgot how much she disliked me. "So these delivery guys are setting the flowers down on my desk and leaving without saying a word, and everyone in the office is crowding around me, watching me open each card. The other women were so jealous—I could totally tell."

"Are you kidding? Of course they were!" Lane said quickly. "So what did the cards say?"

"They didn't say anything, at least not in words. They were pictures. Eric put together a bunch of the pictures he'd taken of me over the years we've been together. How sweet is that?"

"*Soooo* sweet."

Yeah, that was *so* sweet. Damn him. Eric was a good photographer, too. He could probably even make Hillary's scowl look good. Or maybe it was only me she scowled at.

"Then, the last one was a picture of him holding a sign that said: *Will you marry me*?" Squeal. "Isn't that incredible?"

"*So* incredible." Lane was bobbing her head.

Yep, *so* incredible. And I was *so* stupid. A ring under a cup was literally the opposite of incredible.

I've never moved as fast in my life. I lunged forward, my arms outstretched, my eyes on the prize.

Snag! And hallelujah! The ring was back in my hands and the only evidence left behind was a brown ring of coffee on the table. I shoved the proof of my stupidity into my pocket and slipped out of my chair just in time for Hillary to slip into it and shove her hand in Lane's face.

"Oh my God, Laney! Look!" Then lots more girlie squealing,

so much that Lane had to join in. "Look at it! Isn't it beautiful?"

"Oh my God, Carson?"

No, please no. Don't bring me into this. "Yeah, babe?" Oh, fuck. Hadn't I just said my luck was turning? Yep, it just did a 360, or maybe two 360s. Crap.

"Check out Hillary's engagement ring!"

Hillary held out her hand toward me to show off a ring with a diamond so small I had to squint to see it. But the girls were freaking out as if it were the most beautiful thing ever. Was that all it took to make them happy? I'm not a snob, but it looked like something a kid would get after turning in their tickets at an arcade or slipping a quarter into a slot and turning the knob. I'd been in enough jewelry stores in the last month to know that guys in New York didn't bother with stones that small.

"Nice rock, Hillary." I was pretty sure that was an adequate response. I am a man, after all.

"Nice rock?" she said.

Lane looked at me disappointedly.

Okay, maybe it wasn't adequate. But I wasn't going to lie and say it was the most beautiful ring I'd ever seen, especially not while I had a way better one in my pocket at exactly that moment. So I went with the all-occasion, girls-eat-that-shit-up response of, "Almost as pretty as you are."

The cheesy comment seemed to appease both of them, since they went back to their intense discussion about how Eric had proposed. Small rock or not, it sounded a lot better than slipping the ring under a coffee cup. Damn it.

"Hey, Carson," Eric—the motherfucking traitor—said from a few feet behind me. His arms were resting casually at his sides, but he wasn't even trying to hide the shit-eating grin on his face. What the fuck was he so happy about? He'd just ruined my entire day. Maybe my entire life.

Granted, Eric and Hillary had been together for a couple of

years so it wasn't a total surprise. But when you're surrounded by engagement rings, wedding preparations, and prenuptial joy, and you're the only guy who hasn't slipped a ring on his lady's finger, you automatically earn the title of *World's Shittiest Boyfriend.*

"Seriously, man. You *trying* to make me look like an asshole?" Hell yeah, that was whiny. So what? I was stressed out as fuck.

"Yeah," Eric grumbled. "I asked Hillary to spend the rest of her life with me just because I wanted to make you look bad. Working great so far, right?"

"Sorry." I blew out a breath and stuck out the hand that wasn't holding Lane's lukewarm coffee. "Congrats. You guys were meant to be, so...um...yeah, congrats." I didn't know what else to say. Was there some kind of official man protocol in situations like this? If I ever figured it out, I'd give classes—no man should have to go through this unprepared.

Lane was saying something unintelligible to the male ear, so I only got bits. And glares. How could two small women throw that many glares? Pointy ones too, like Samurai stars.

"I need a drink." I said it without thought, but it was a great idea. "Champagne!" I looked at Lane and Hillary for confirmation. "This kind of news deserves to be celebrated with something stronger than coffee, doesn't it?"

Hillary squinted and looked up to the left. Nope, definitely ceiling there, no answer.

But I got her hesitation. She was probably thinking about their finances and how expensive weddings were. "Our treat."

"Then hell yes!" Hillary squealed. No judgment behind using the word to describe almost everything she says—she's just easily excited. Whenever I see her, at least. And I don't think it has anything to do with her and my unfortunate past. That no one was ever going to mention again.

"It's a little early for Champagne, isn't it?" Eric asked.

"True." It was probably the first time Hillary's smile had fallen all day. "And I was so excited, I didn't even eat lunch."

"I guess we should get some dinner to go along with the Champagne." Then I added, "Also our treat."

"Double yes!" Hillary jumped out of the chair, went to Eric, and whispered something into his ear.

At the same time, Lane mouthed, "*Our* treat?" to me.

I shrugged. "Think of it like *our* engagement gift to you."

Hillary's carefree, "Our first engagement gift!" completely covered Eric's shy, "Thanks, Carson."

Lane's gaze didn't move—it intensified. She knew me too damn well. But she didn't call me on it in front of her friends. *Our* friends, I guess.

One of the most bizarre parts of being in a relationship was everything and everyone had become *ours*. Friends, apartments, family. Although why anyone would want to claim partial ownership of my family, I'd never understand. For the most part, I didn't mind it. Occasionally I liked it. Especially when referring to *our* bed, *our* bathtub, or *our* favorite position.

Lane just didn't like to think of my money as *ours*. She didn't want to feel like a gold digger or something equally stupid. What I tried to explain to her, and what she never understood, was that *I* was the one getting the gold. I didn't care about money. I cared about the feisty little pot of gold I went to sleep with every night and woke up next to every morning.

I shrugged and went to go dump Lane's cup in the trash, wondering what I would've done if she'd picked it up like I'd expected her to.

Would she have squealed when she saw the ring I'd spent weeks searching for? Just to make sure it deserved to be worn by my amazing woman.

Would she have said yes?

3

LANEY

I WATCHED Carson tip back another glass of expensive Champagne out of the corner of my eye, wondering what was wrong with him and when I should bring it up. During the last-minute engagement celebration for Hillary and Eric probably wasn't the best time. Luckily, Carson and I were roomies, which gave me lots of time to wonder what had been distracting him so much.

I'd been noticing it more and more lately. At the café earlier, he'd been somewhere else mentally, which was really unlike him. One of the things I loved most about him was his ability to ignore everything but the present. Actually, make that one of the things I both loved *and* hated about him.

But complaining about my next-to-perfect life seemed a bit too narcissistic. Everything had been amazing with Carson and I since the very beginning and, after a few rough patches that had mostly centered around his inexperience in living with someone he actually liked—i.e. someone he wasn't related to—I couldn't be happier.

Okay, that was a lie. I *could* be happier, but I didn't know how. Some small part of me felt like something was missing. I just couldn't figure out what it was. Maybe what bothered Carson was that he knew something was bothering *me*? Great, neither of us knew what the hell was going on. Time for some serious relationship evaluation. Internally, of course, because relationship evaluation was the one thing Carson completely sucked at. Thankfully, he was good at all the other parts, so it didn't matter. You don't need to assess a situation that's really great, right?

He loved me. I loved him. We never fought and—

Maybe that was it. Other than my parents, couples fought. It was totally normal, healthy even. What wasn't normal was for two people to be around each other so much and never fight. Maybe that's what Carson and I needed.

As stupid as the idea was, it also made sense considering who our parental role models were. I'd never learned how to fight, and Carson had never learned how to fight without things getting violent. Stick us together and you had a non-confrontational powder keg ready to blow up any second.

Pick your battles suddenly meant something different. Maybe I needed to commit, pick something small so we could practice fighting. Then, once we figured it out, I would choose a larger conflict. This was potentially the worst idea I'd ever had, but how else could we learn? And we had to learn—that I was sure of.

Hillary and Eric fought all the time, and they were engaged. Carson's brother and his fiancée argued occasionally, I was sure, and they were getting married in a few days. Even my parents fought—not loudly and never when they thought I could hear, but I always knew when it was coming. My mom would clench her jaw and find something to busy herself with, and my dad would send me to bed. The first time I realized that was code for *you need to leave so we can argue* was when he'd told me it was bedtime at four o'clock in the afternoon.

And the most damning, if that's the right way to look at it, was that I'd never fought with any of my ex-boyfriends. And those relationships were doomed. So, yeah, damning *was* the right way to look at it. I couldn't let Carson's and my relationship go that route. Being able to fight properly, and make up properly, were two things healthy couples did. Especially because I knew eventually we'd have something big to fight about and, if we weren't ready, we'd lose everything we'd worked so hard for.

Ever since we finally realized we wanted to be together, the only stuff we fought about were things that could be fixed with a joke or a kiss. Taking the last of the coffee or leaving the toilet seat up weren't exactly declarations of war.

Carson caught me staring and leaned closer, setting his glass down so he could brush my hair behind my ear. I don't care how many times he touched me, that rush of adrenaline would never go away.

He kissed my cheek and whispered, "You want another drink, gorgeous?"

I didn't answer right away because I knew as soon as I did, he'd go get it for me. And I wanted to enjoy the warmth of his breath a little longer.

"Another round?" Eric asked loudly.

Hillary answered immediately. "Hell, yeah, my almost-husband."

"Can't see that getting old anytime soon," I teased. Over the last half hour, she'd been calling him a different variation of it every time she spoke. Almost-husband, it's-about-time-you-asked-man, soon-to-be-groom, or future Mr. Miller—which he balked at. Evidently, he wouldn't be taking her name after they got married.

I laughed and felt Carson pull away. Something was definitely wrong. Maybe I wouldn't have to pick a fight, after all. Maybe it would happen organically. Damn, I hoped we were ready for it.

I dumped my bag on the table I'd designed for our apartment. *Our* apartment. I would never get used to that. Aside from the fact I'd never be able to afford this place on my own—not that he let me pay for any of it, of course—it just felt weird to think of something that had been his for so long as partially mine. I adored living here, though.

The whole place was a reclaimed-wood showcase for my designs now. To the point where I'd started refusing to sell him anything else because my shins and hip bones were already bruised from walking into tables, stools, and desks all the time. Plus, I was trying to build a name for myself as an artist, which meant people actually had to *see* the art to be able to buy it. Thankfully, I'd been able to get a larger warehouse space, one with a back room Carson wasn't allowed in, where I could hide any new pieces I'd finished working on.

My suitcases were packed and ready for our trip to Tahiti for Carson's brother Hayden's marriage to his incredible fiancée Andi. Since I'd never actually been to an island, I may have over-done it. I wasn't sure what was appropriate attire, but you couldn't go wrong with layers, right? Lots and lots of layers. And lingerie because Carson loved it. And way too many shoes. We were only going to be there for seven days—two before the wedding and five after, so we could explore by ourselves and pretend we were shipwrecked. Maybe I wouldn't need all those layers, after all. Or any, actually.

If I knew Carson, he'd make me close my eyes and imagine our ship going down in a huge storm. As the waves got bigger and tossed our poor little vessel around, he'd shake me for authenticity. Then he'd start tearing my clothes off—because, obviously, that would happen in a storm—until I was in my underwear. We'd spend the next five days living off coconuts and mangos. Oh, man, now I'd screwed myself. If he didn't do that,

I'd be so disappointed. I'd probably spend the entire trip pouting and horny. Speaking of...

I turned around when he was right behind me and slid my hands over his shoulders. "Are you still in the mood to celebrate?"

He didn't move, like, not even to grope me. "What's there to celebrate?" he snapped. Then he moved—to create empty space between us. For the first time ever.

"What's going on?"

"I just want to go to bed." He brushed by me and headed toward the bedroom.

"That's what I was hinting at," I mumbled, knowing our motivations were completely different. Totally clueless as to *why,* though. "Carson, what's wrong?"

He turned in the doorway, resting an arm on one side of the jamb, rubbing his lips together but not looking at me. "Do you ever wonder if you'd be better off with someone like Eric? Someone...with a little insight into what he wants out of life?"

Oh, shit. Everything had been going so well. Too well. For a second, I felt like I'd just stepped out of my body and was watching the two of us stand there, fifteen feet away from each other, not understanding a goddamn thing. And for another second, I wondered if I was witnessing the beginning of the end. When two people stopped being able to understand each other or express what was going on.

When two people started falling apart.

4

LANEY

NOT US. Never us. I snapped back into my body and stomped toward him, pumping my arms as if the room were the length of a football field. "No. No, Carson, no. Just no."

"No what, Lane? No, I'm not allowed to ask? Or no, I'm not allowed to feel?"

"No, you're not *supposed* to feel that. And no, you shouldn't *need* to ask." I stopped a foot away from him, my hands gripping my pants. "Where is this coming from? I thought we were having fun. I thought we were okay."

"Okay?" he asked skeptically. "Is that all you want? An okay life with an okay guy in an okay apartment?"

"First off, no one would ever describe this apartment as 'okay.'" The joke fell flat so I tried again. "I love you. And I love our life together. Don't you?

"You know the answer to that question," he said. "It's never going to change."

"Then what's going on?"

"What's going on? Well, my brother is getting hitched... again. *This* time to someone he actually loves. He has a great house, his business is doing really well, and as soon as they get back from their wedding, he and Andi will probably start popping out mini Handi's."

Normally, I loved hearing his shortcut expression to describe his brother and fiancée. Almost as much as I loved that he thought of us as "Carney." Did it mean he'd call our kids Carnies? Wasn't a big fan of that possibility. Just like I wasn't a big fan of the intensity of this entire conversation.

"Eric and Hillary are engaged," he continued, "and are already looking for a house together. Everyone around us is planning out their future, Lane. But we've never even talked about it. I don't even know if you want kids, or if you want to stay in San Francisco, or if you even *want* to get married." He took a breath. "Why don't you ever talk about our future, babe? Women talk about that shit all the time. Even when they don't have a guy. But you don't. You never have. Why not?"

I scratched my head, maybe to get my brain working again. Because I didn't know. He was right—we didn't talk about that stuff. We talked about everything...except where our relationship was headed. He made the occasional joke about it—kids, making an honest woman out of me, those kinds of things—but we'd never talked about it seriously. I had a five-year plan for my career, but not for us. I guess I'd just been so worried about our relationship changing I'd never really considered that change isn't always a *bad* thing. And it was inevitable anyway.

While I knew Carson was so much better than all the frogs I'd been with, I still couldn't forget how hurt I'd been when my future plans had proven to be so far from reality. *Expectations* and *happy endings* were still dirty words, scary phrases. Just like *What's that crawling on your shoulder?* or *politician*.

"Do you not think I'm going to be part of it?" he asked softly. "Is that why?"

I inhaled only halfway, my body refusing to function, just like my mouth. All I could force out was a long, pathetic-sounding, "No." I stuttered, tried to formulate thought, but nothing happened. It was one of those moments, those horrible moments in a movie when you yell at the screen and scream, "Say something!" to the character.

A couple of words. That's all it would take. And everything might be able to go back to normal.

But this was so unexpected, I didn't know how to respond. No words appeared in my head. No useful ones, anyway.

I wiped my hand over my face. "I don't know what to say other than *no*, that's not why."

"Do you want to be with me?"

I nodded so fast I had to step backwards to catch myself before I fell over.

He sighed. "You're drunk."

I grabbed his arm as he turned away. "I'm not drunk. I'm just...I didn't expect to have this conversation, so I'm at a loss for what to tell you. But you're wrong. About everything. I want to be with you. I don't know why we don't talk about it. But we can."

I couldn't tell if he believed me. The look on his face showed me nothing other than that he was hurting. And somehow, some way, it was my fault. All the things I didn't say or hadn't said for reasons I didn't know. Oh, shit. I was seriously blowing this.

"Can we talk about it?" I asked softly.

He blew out a breath and then reached out to me, cradling my cheek in his hand. "Tomorrow, okay? I'm not up to it tonight."

I held his hand to my face, not wanting him to go.

He kissed my forehead and whispered, "Maybe I'm going nuts. I don't know. Let's go to bed. We'll have plenty of time to talk on the flight tomorrow."

Without any other choice, I followed him into the bedroom, holding his hand tightly in mine.

How fucking ironic. I'd decided a good fight was what we needed. *Be careful what you wish for.*

I wasn't ready for this. The idea had been to start small—little baby arguments we could handle before we tried tackling anything harder. This was emotional and deep, *too* emotional and *too* deep. We weren't prepared for it.

And I would never have picked this battle.

5

LANEY

I COULDN'T SLEEP. I didn't know how much rest Carson got either. Our bed had never felt so big before. Normally, we shared the middle, leaving both sides empty. But not tonight. Tonight, we each had a side. We still held hands as we pretended to sleep, but there was so much damn space between us.

I wanted to say something, to talk about what the hell had happened, but what good would it do if *he* didn't want to?

And the truth was, I still didn't know what to tell him. Why hadn't we ever talked about the future? Because the present was so great? We'd spent hours talking about our pasts—good and bad—and he knew me better than anyone ever had. He understood me better than *I* did sometimes. That kind of freaked me out, actually. Especially now. Maybe he saw something I couldn't. He was right—it *was* weird I never talked about babies or a house in the suburbs. He'd never even met my parents. He'd spoken to them on the phone a few times—a quick "Hello" or "Hope we can visit soon"—but for one reason or another, I hadn't introduced him to them.

He was just so different than they were, so different than the kind of man they thought I'd end up with. *Hoped* I'd end up with. On paper, at least. I knew once they got to know him a little, they'd fall in love with him just the way I had. See beyond the tattoos, the inherited wealth, the sarcasm, the lack of a filter and any normalcy in his life. I wished I could introduce them like they did on *The Voice*—judge him before seeing him or finding out about his past. Judge him by who he was *now*: an amazingly thoughtful man who ran a children's charity, for goodness sake. What parents wouldn't approve of that? If only I could somehow keep his past troubles and his current mischievousness from them.

And I knew he'd love them, once he saw past their lifestyle, their expectations, their...normalcy. The way they judged people who chose to live in the moment and take risks. People who had pasts worthy of forgetting.

I finally fell asleep around two-thirty, still wondering which part of my life I was really trying to hide.

6

CARSON

LAST NIGHT HAD BEEN TRAGIC. After being a nutcase all day long, I'd thought there was no way things could get worse after the botched proposal. Boy, had I underestimated my stupidity.

Number one: Putting the ring under her cup and proposing in a café filled with strangers. *Si romantique.*

I'd chicken-shitted myself into thinking five minutes of planning would be enough. As long as she got a great ring and I got a "Yes," nothing else mattered. But according to Hillary's *numerous* accounts of how thoughtful and romantic Eric had been when he'd asked, how she couldn't wait to tell everyone she knew, and everyone she didn't—including her future grandkids—evidently a proper proposal had to be over-the-top romantic and involve at least three candles and two kinds of flowers.

Number two: Watching Lane get so excited about Hillary and Eric's engagement had made it abundantly clear she wanted that. That was good, right? I mean, an hour before, I'd been ready to pop the question. Well, *ready* wasn't what I'd been, but I'd been about to do it anyway.

But as the night drew on and the Champagne bottles emptied, I felt Lane distance herself from me. And then, when

Hillary made a joke about what was taking us so long to get hitched, Lane's light-speed response felt like a stab to my gut.

"Oh, pleeeeaaase. You're talking about Carson Bennett, Hillary."

What the fuck did that mean? Hadn't I brought Lane into my life, my mind, my fucking heart enough to prove myself? Told her without words that this was serious shit and that I was all-in and determined to make it last? What the fuck else could I do to prove it to her?

And to think, when she'd said that, I'd actually had her fucking ring in my pocket.

That's when it hit me—Eric and Hillary had their whole lives planned out. So did Hayden and Andi. They all knew what their futures looked like. They saw them, believed in them, fucking *talked* about them.

There I was, ready to steal some candles, get down on one knee, and beg her to make it official, when I realized we had never *once* spoken about what happened next. We'd never daydreamed or over-examined or gotten completely delusional about all the shit couples did. China patterns and kid names and whose family we'd drag ourselves to for holidays.

And shit, that was another thing. My family was one big ball of fuck up. If I could, I would've pretended I was an orphan. I guess I'd still claim I had a brother, but Lane had spent time with my mother and my wicked stepsister. She had broken bread with them, knew all their hang-ups, their vices, their evil, evil ways. I'd always figured I was lucky not to have to go to San Diego and spend time with Lane's parents, small talking while keeping my hands and thoughts to myself. Now that good fortune seemed like a red flag. *She hasn't introduced you to her parents because she's still not sure you'll be around long enough to bother, idiot.*

Everything twisted up in my head. All her attempts to save me from the whole meeting-the-parents torture had been a big fucking sign. The kind of sign you passed five times a day and never noticed until you accidentally tripped over it and were forced to look at it more closely. I was finally compelled to pick it up, dust it off, and read it. Realize it had been there the whole fucking time.

I should've stopped and read it sooner. But no, I'd been skipping along like a happy idiot, wrapped up in warm and cozy feelings without realizing Lane and I were stuck. So stuck there was a good chance we'd never make it any farther than we already were.

When I woke up, Lane was sitting next to me, her legs tucked under her, naked and staring at me as if she'd been doing it a while. Her hair was messy, probably from tossing and turning and worrying all night. I rubbed my eyes and stretched, wondering who would make the first move.

Women were better at talking, so I waited for her to start. Then I waited a little longer. And a little longer. Seemed like forever but was probably only about a minute or so.

Fuck this. I didn't want to feel disconnected from her for another second.

I pulled her down to me, wrapped my arms around her and held on tightly, feeling the warmth of her breath on my chest. I didn't feel her tears drip onto me, but I knew they were there— her breath sped up and her body jerked with each one. So I held on tighter.

"I'm not going to let either of us ruin this," I said firmly. "I'm not. Understand?"

Her nose poked me as she nodded. There was a possibility I was smothering her, but I couldn't let go. Not yet. Not until I knew she understood.

"I don't care if you have doubts or are looking for a way out. I don't care. Well, obviously I care, but I'm not going to let it matter. I'm going to fix this." As soon as I figured out what it was.

I let her up for air because the whole till-death-do-us-part bit wasn't going to happen until we were old, wrinkly, and I couldn't get it up without a little blue pill.

As if she'd read my mind—or my body—she threw her leg over me and slid down until my cock—which wouldn't need a blue pill anytime soon—prodded her core.

Both of us groaned at the same time, for the same reason, and it wasn't a good one. But we survived.

After an impressively quick reach-and-grab from the night-stand drawer, Lane tore the condom wrapper in half, tossed it over her shoulder, and rolled that rubber bastard right down my cock in record time.

Then she guided my morning wood inside her and pressed down on me, both of us sighing long and low. I would never get tired of feeling her wrapped around me. I swear, if we wouldn't get arrested for it, I'd wear her around all day, every day, constantly rocking her up and down my cock. Never coming, never stopping, just enjoying the sweetness of our connection.

She lifted up just a tiny, torturous bit and then slid back down, grinding her hips against mine. No idea how she managed it, but somehow she found the focus to speak. Unfortunately, that meant I somehow had to find the focus to listen.

"I want a small wedding. Nothing fancy—just our friends, your family and mine. I want my dad to walk me down the aisle."

"Yeah," I groaned. I really didn't want to think about her father while my cock was inside her, but I let her keep talking. I needed to hear this.

"We're going to need a big house." Her breath caught. "With a big shop so I can work from home..." She closed her eyes as if she wanted every cell in her body to focus only on where our skin touched.

"What else?"

"I want a...a..." Her fingernails dug into my chest each time I pushed my hips up and pulled hers down.

"What else?" I repeated.

"A pool. So we can go skinny-dipping." She rocked her hips faster, more intensely, her forehead tightening as she worked toward her end.

"And a big fence so the neighbors can't watch us fuck in the water."

"Yes!" she said, maybe about the fence, maybe about the way I slid my hand between us to make sure she would come before I did.

"What else do you want, Lane?" I sat up. It meant I couldn't be as deep as I wanted to be, but I needed more of our skin to touch. She threw her arms around my shoulders, her breasts pressed to my chest, her uneven breaths hot against my neck.

"Just you. Forever. Nothing else matters."

I spun both of us over so she was under me, so I could be in control. Speed, depth, angle.

I was a smart enough man to have paid close attention to exactly what my woman needed when she was this close. And I was a skilled enough man to give it to her. My only job was to get her over the line before her pleasure plateaued, she got frustrated with her own body, and gave up on it. No greater orgasm killer than frustration. For her, at least. I could've come even if a mountain fell on us.

But...oh shit! Her muscles clenched around my cock like a vise.

"Not fair," I growled. "You can't...do that."

"I can do whatever...ah...I want...to you." She knew how

close I was to losing it. And, damn her, she used my weakness against me.

"Seriously, Lane. Stop, or I'm gonna...ahhh..."

Luckily I knew all her signs too—the long, shaky inhalation, the raised eyebrows, the eyes that begged me to finish her off. And then a moment of absolute silence before...

Oh, here she comes.

Just in time too. When we kissed, it felt true, real, perfect. We lost it together—my orgasm hitting seconds after hers started.

I let go inside her, my fingers digging into the mattress as I arched my back, and added a loud, "Fuuuuuck."

I struggled not to fall asleep right on top of her and forced myself to keep rocking into her until her final moan had ended.

I *lived* for that final moan. The one that lasted for a minute, maybe even a minute and a half. Or maybe it was fifteen seconds but just felt like more. Because right after, Lane always went limp and collapsed wherever she was. Always. No matter what position we were in.

I doubt she even knew she did it. All I knew was she needed me to catch her.

7

CARSON

AFTER A DEEP, lingering kiss broken up by some heavy breathing, I flopped onto the bed beside her. I weakly pulled a few strands of her hair out of my mouth then dealt with the condom, tossing it into the trash can next to the bed.

It took another minute to catch our breaths. At least that's what I told myself was the reason neither of us said anything. We turned to each other at the same time, then spoke simultaneously. "I'm sorry."

Before she could say anything else untrue, I said, "You don't need to be sorry, Lane. It was my fault. I shouldn't have brought it up."

She pressed up on her hands and looked down at me. "Maybe the way you did could've been better, but you were right to bring it up. I don't want us to keep things from each other."

I sighed. "Okay, then if we're really coming clean, I should probably tell you that you look weird with beard-burn on your cheeks." I rubbed the stubble on my chin that had caused it. "Cute but weird. Does it hurt?"

I saw a flicker of a smile. Then an eye roll. Then a bigger smile.

"Not as much as when it's on the inside of my thighs. Maybe you need to shave more often."

"I'm getting you a thigh spreader for your birthday—problem solved." I smiled. "Actually, this bed would look great with wrist and ankle straps, don't you think?"

"So we're good?"

I shook my head. "Frozen yogurt is good. Sleeping in is good. You are...incredible. So, even taking off a few points for when we add me to the combo, I'd say that still leaves us around fantastic." Not quite the right word, but it would do. "But as much as I hate to admit it, we should probably...*talk* more."

"We'll have plenty of time to talk on the airplane." Her eyelids fell, dropping like a kid trying not to fall asleep in class. She must have been exhausted.

I glanced at the alarm clock, then back at her. Oh shit, I had to get moving. Since Hayden had taken Andi on a trip around Asia to distract her before their wedding, he'd made me promise to do something for him before Lane and I left the states. I'd forgotten to do it yesterday, and it needed to be done.

I sighed, gave Lane one last quick-ish kiss, and hauled my sorry ass out of bed. Lane mumbled when she felt the mattress move.

Normally, to do our part for the environment, we showered together. I wasn't sure how much water it actually saved since we usually got distracted and took way longer to finish than if we'd been solo.

In my defense, I was never allowed to have bath toys as a child. Renee complained that they splashed water everywhere and it would ruin the floor. So Lane was helping me work through those horrible memories of bath time by letting me play with *her*.

When I came out, my disappointment over Lane not joining

me was overcome by the sight of her still lying in bed like a sexually sated and unconscious snow angel. Before she could ruin the image by drooling, I quickly threw some clothes on and gave her a light kiss on her forehead.

"Be back as soon as I can."

"Wait," she said groggily, propping up on her elbows. "Where are you going? It's still early."

"I promised Hayden I'd run by their house to check something out before we left."

"Don't be late."

"Yes, ma'am." The car would pick us up to take us to the airport in two hours. No way would my errand take that long.

An hour and fifteen minutes later, I was still wandering around Hayden and Andi's house with my mouth hanging open. The contractor Hayden hired had turned the house where Andi grew up into a home where they could grow old.

Sean, the contractor, gave me a tour of the bathrooms, the kitchen, and the living room. Only thing left to check was the completely new addition to the house—the master suite.

Sean pointed to the remote he'd given me at the beginning of the tour. "Now, if you press the button that says *Master*—"

"A submissive woman will magically appear to cater to my every whim?" I joked.

"No," he said, scratching his metrosexual facial hair. He didn't share my sense of humor. Or anyone's sense of humor, for that matter. Being trendy prevented it, I think. "Pressing the button notifies the system which room you want to control."

"Yeah. Control in the bedroom is definitely key. Don't want to be a two-minute man, am I right?"

He ignored me. "Just press the button."

I did.

"Now, hit the big light button. *That* one." Wow. He should have been a kindergarten teacher—without his help, who *knew* which button I would've thought was big and said *Light* on it. "Now, like in every other room, the system will be biometrically set to only recognize Hayden's and Andi's vocal registers. Everyone else will have to use the controller. They can program it when they get back."

"Right."

He acted like I was supposed to be impressed by all of this. As if I've never watched the SYFY channel or seen Minority Report.

I pushed the music button—it was a medium-sized button with the word *Music* on it—then pretended to press a bunch of others just to mess with him.

"Quick! Where's the knob to change the station?" I needed something to save me from the smooth new age jazz or whatever filled my ears. "Do people actually have sex to this music?"

"There are over 1,500 different satellite stations available." He tried to take the remote from me. Then grudgingly pointed to an arrow pointing to the right that I would've eventually figured out on my own.

"Of course there are." I sighed. "That it?"

Of course it wasn't. There were buttons and voice controls to dim the lights, control the alarm clock, change the room temperature, and adjust the heat of the mattress. Maybe it could even read you a story or jack you off before bed. Unfortunately my time to dwell was long over.

"Got it. Looks great. I'll inform my brother." Shit, I'd forgotten to take the video I'd promised Hayden I would shoot. I checked the clock on my phone and saw a message from Lane:

'Where are you??? We leave in thirty minutes!'

Oh shit. "I gotta go, Sean. Like, ten minutes ago. But I need you to take a quick video tour of the place and email it to me so I can show Hayden when I see him."

"If you'd told me earlier, I could've taught you how to use the house monitoring app."

"Sean, the *last* thing I want on my phone is a way to see what's happening in my brother's bedroom." Thankfully Andi was a computer genius. She would set up additional, unhackable security as soon as the surprise was unveiled to her. "Just a short video of the place will do. Thanks." I ran for the door, wondering if I would be able to get out of here without the remote. "And, Sean? Seriously, you do awesome work, man. It's amazing."

Huh. Guess I was wrong. He *did* know how to smile. Then he looked down at the remote, pressed a button, and the front door opened all by itself.

"I bow to your skills, man."

As I sped home, I thought about how lucky my brother was. Or maybe it wasn't luck. That asshat had worked his hat off to get what he had, and every day since, he put in the effort to keep it. Finding a woman who'd taught him it was okay to want things he'd never dreamed he'd have was his due for putting up with everybody else's family shit for so long.

I adored Andi. She accepted my brother as he was and, just by being herself, had made him even better. No two people were more deserving. And this surprise he'd planned for her—turning the home she already loved into something they'd love even more—couldn't have been a more perfect symbol of their relationship.

Fuck. Was that what I should do for Lane? Give her the proposal, wedding, and future that symbolized *our* relationship? Not sure if that made me more or less nervous.

What we had was perfect most of the time because it was

easy, intense, and full of laughs. Actually, I could use the same description for our sex life.

Nah, proposing during sex was probably a big no-no. And, sadly, she'd never go for having sex *during* our wedding. At least our future would be filled with a lot of it.

A future that was easy, intense, full of laughs, and almost as much sex. Yep, that sounded perfect.

8

LANEY

I LAID my light green bridesmaid dress down on the bed next to Carson's best man outfit. I planned to pack them at the very last minute. I didn't *think* they'd wrinkle in a garment bag, but I wasn't sure. Ironing wasn't a skill in my tool box, so to speak. So not putting them into something where they'd be bunched up until it was absolutely necessary seemed like a reasonable thing to do.

"Cutting it a little close there, aren't you?" I said as Carson threw the door open and ran straight into the bedroom to get ready. Because he had exactly *nothing* packed, despite my frequent reminders over the past two weeks.

"Plenty of time." He grabbed the suitcase I'd put out for him eons ago and headed into the walk-in closet.

"Yeah, like five extra minutes."

He flinched and spun around when he realized I'd followed him. I wish I knew why he'd been so distracted or anxious lately.

That's when I saw the white plastic bag he was shoving into his suitcase. When did he have time to go shopping?

"Yep, plenty of time." He reached out to grab my hand and

pull me into him, sliding his hand onto my ass and squeezing. "Thanks for this morning, by the way. I needed that."

"Me too."

It's funny how sex can bring people closer. Not that I missed the literal meaning of the idea, but the emotional component still came as a surprise to me, even after the countless times Carson and I had done it. But being with someone I truly loved and was 110 percent sure loved me just as much was still kind of new to me. Having a guy on top of you, or inside you, didn't automatically provide that experience. But with Carson, I knew he wasn't holding anything back. Every movement he made, every word he groaned, gave him away.

This morning wasn't just sex for either of us. It was a moment of shared vulnerability, openness, and acceptance I'd never had with anyone before him. And since I *knew* he'd never had it before, it was as if we were both experiencing the same thing, feeling the same emotional component.

Actually he probably wasn't thinking anything in the moment. If he were, it had probably been something like, "Ahhh...oooh...gooooood."

"I'm coming," I whispered.

"Huh?"

Shit. I'd said that last part out loud. I shook my head. "I mean the *car* we ordered is coming. Soon. It's coming soon." Meh cover. Thankfully, he didn't question it.

I raised onto my tiptoes and kissed him, planning it to be quick so he could finish packing. But Carson lived in the moment. And at this moment, he wasn't thinking about what to pack or how long it would take us to get through airport security. He matched my quick kiss and raised me a scorching connection of tongues and heat until I'd forgotten everything else too.

"Knock it off!" I pushed away from him. "We don't have time for any of that, mister."

"Fine," he grumbled. "I can wait until after the captain has turned off the fasten seatbelt sign."

While I threw together a quick breakfast for us, Carson shoved stuff into a bag and got ready to go.

When my phone buzzed, letting us know our ride was downstairs waiting, Carson was dressed and I was running around trying to figure out what I'd forgotten to pack. Because, obviously, I'd forgotten *something*.

"Was the wedding switched to a clothing-optional event?" Carson said, stuffing the last bite of the breakfast burrito into his mouth.

"What are you talking about?" I followed his gaze to the bedroom, toward the wedding attire I'd laid out about three minutes ago and then had promptly forgotten about. "See? I knew I'd forget something."

"So we aren't doing it naked?" he asked, frowning melodramatically. "Bummer. Hopes dashed. Disappointment overwhelming."

"Disaster averted." I took one last look at my dress and his outfit before zipping up the garment bag, willing them not to wrinkle. The dress was gorgeous and would flow beautifully with the island breeze, but I would've gone with a more formal look for the men. Especially because Carson looks painfully gorgeous in a tux.

Carson grabbed our luggage, I locked the apartment door, and we ran to get the elevator. It was a short ride down, but it gave me enough time to obsess a little more.

Specifically, I thought about how weird it was that it had taken me this long to start daydreaming about what I would want at my wedding. Until I'd met Carson, it was my favorite fantasy. Well, that's not fair to Carson. He hadn't been the reason

I'd stopped daydreaming about it. The asshole *before* Carson could have all the blame for that one.

I really hadn't thought about getting married in a long time. I wished I could say it was because Carson gave me all kinds of new, better, and naughtier fantasies—which was entirely true—but I worked alone all day long. Plenty of time to imagine the really dirty stuff *and* the traditionally girlie stuff. But I hadn't. Why not?

Fear. Wasn't that always the reason people avoided something? In my case, it was probably fear of falling into the same trap I'd fallen into before...a bunch of times. Stuck in the trap until I got dumped. *Way* past the moment I'd realized the guy was a jerk. But I'd already committed to the idea. It was too late to back out.

Yes, eventually I realized how stupid that was. It just took a lot longer than I wish it had.

Before Carson, I was fantasizing about being Mrs. Whoever by the third date. Everything was different this time around, better, smarter, healthier. I needed it to work. I think I'd been so busy trying to make sure I wasn't the same stupid person I used to be, that I'd never really allowed myself to think of anything beyond that.

I was momentarily blinded by sunlight when we stepped out of the building. By the time I could see again, Carson was already shaking hands with the driver of our car.

I walked toward the door Carson must have opened for me. As soon as I felt leather under my ass, I closed my eyes and waited. Once Carson had put all our bags into the trunk and slid into the seat beside me, I scooted into the center seat so I could rest my head on his shoulder.

We made it through airport security and to the gate with about two minutes to spare. Carson was dragging all the bags and wouldn't accept my help with them, so I ran ahead to make sure they didn't shut the door.

"See?" he said as we took our seats in first class. "Plenty of time."

9

LANEY

As soon as the plane took off and I'd had two glasses of complimentary Champagne—seriously, I'd never get used to how rich people live—Carson drained his glass, pressed both our seats into the reclining position, and pulled me in close, resting his chin on my head.

A few minutes later, his breath slowed and his hand relaxed in mine. I guess he'd gotten even less sleep than I had last night and he needed it now.

I hated to say it, but I was kind of glad Carson had crashed so quickly and stayed asleep most of the trip. I just wasn't ready to talk about anything too serious—I needed a chance to figure out some stuff for myself.

I dozed a little, wiggled out of his grip, and read the in-flight magazine, glancing over at him after every few pages to make sure he was okay. He twitched a lot, his brows came together, and he mouthed things I couldn't make out.

By the time I'd figured out what overpriced and useless things I wanted to buy from the catalogue very generously offered by the airline, the flight attendant announced they'd be around for one last round of drinks before we landed.

Hmm... I really wanted another glass of Champagne, especially considering how much Carson must have paid for these seats. But if I did, I'd pee my pants. With my luck, the flight attendant would announce over the speaker system that more warm towels were needed in first class because *someone* had a bit too much bubbly.

I unclipped my seatbelt and tried to get past Carson without waking him up. With whatever kind of sixth sense he had wherever my ass was concerned, he woke up right when it was in front of his face and grabbed it. I squealed and looked around at the other passengers, hoping no one had seen him grope me and yank me into his lap.

"Let go, Carson. I really don't want to pee on you."

He wiped his eyes and looked at me, confused. I think he'd forgotten where we were. I used the seat back in front of me to pull myself off him and walked down the aisle as quickly as I could. My legs were stiff from sitting so long. I must have looked really first-classy teetering down the aisle with my thighs squeezed together and my feet apart so I didn't accidentally fall into someone else's lap.

Once I'd avoided an international embarrassment, I went back to my seat. The flight attendant was bent over, talking to Carson. Or maybe she wasn't talking. Maybe she was just showing him her tits—I couldn't be sure. That was one thing I hated about being with him—women seemed to not understand or not care that he was taken.

It had occurred to me on numerous occasions they must think I was his sister or something, because they hit on him either right in front of me or as soon as my back was turned. And it really kind of pissed me off. Whatever happened to the girl code? Wasn't it international?

"Excuse me." I tapped the woman on the shoulder and rolled my eyes, my other hand bracing on the back of the seat next to me. "That's my seat"—I pointed past her—"and that's my man." I pointed to Carson. "You'd know better than me, but don't property rights go beyond international boundaries?"

"I...um..." Huh. Evidently embarrassed stuttering is universal.

I looked at Carson. "Sorry for calling you my property."

He shrugged. "I thought it was hot. Although it would've been hotter if you'd claimed me first and *then* your seat." He reached around the attendant to take my hand. "Do you want anything else to drink?"

The woman's smile tightened but she backed off, and I wasn't ashamed to admit feeling a large amount of superiority when he pulled me into his lap.

"I'd love some coffee."

"Good idea. I'll have some, too."

"Then I'll go get you some," she snapped and wandered off.

I was definitely going to make Carson share his coffee with me. At least *his* wouldn't have spit in it.

"I can't believe she hit on you!" I crawled off him and into my own seat, straightening my top. "I was already using the damn bathroom. Where did she plan on fucking you?"

"She wasn't hitting on me."

"Liar."

He smirked. "Actually, my love, we were talking about how long you and I have been together. She thought we looked great together. So if she really *was* hitting on me, she wanted something a lot hotter than just her and I. But if there's a way all three of us could fit in one of those bathrooms..." He raised his hand as if to wave her back over.

"Pervert." I smacked him as he laughed. "So I owe her an apology for being a bitch to her."

"Maybe a little one."

I smacked him again, and he laughed again.

"Hey!" He rubbed where I'd hit him, as if it had actually hurt him. "I meant a little *apology*, not a little bitch."

"Sure you did. Just for that, you're not getting your threesome."

"I'll live." His lips brushed the top of my head when I leaned in close to kiss the horrible injury I'd caused him. "I have to work my ass off to keep *you* happy. No way I'm up to adding anyone else in. Plus, fair's fair. If I wanted to invite another woman into our bed, you'd be allowed to invite another guy. And that'll never be up for negotiation."

"Even for my birthday?" I teased.

"Hell, no." One eyebrow bounced while he spoke. With Carson, that was like seeing a neon billboard that said "DANGER" in all caps. "I have something much better planned for your birthday."

"An orgy?"

He grimaced. "Fuck no! I can't even stomach that in porn. Do you have any idea how sticky you'd get at one of those things? And what fluids would *make* you sticky?" He shivered dramatically. "Quick, talk about something else."

"Okay, let's talk about your brother."

"Agh!" He clenched his eyes shut. "You can't go from an orgy discussion straight to my brother, Lane. Have you no pity on a man's overactive imagination? It takes at least three steps to get a man to stop thinking about sex—you know that!"

"I do now. Okay, orgy...stickiness...um..." I guess it really *was* hard being a man. "Tape...video..."

"Not helping—video and sex go hand in hand."

"Everything and sex goes hand in hand with you."

"Not anymore. I haven't needed to use my hand on myself in eons. Although they get plenty of action on your beautiful body, and— Damn it. That's not helping. Say something totally unsexy."

"You have a superhuman ability to connect every word in the English language to sex." But I tried again, because he was so cute when he squirmed. "Okay, where were we? Um...video... wedding video...are Andi and Hayden having anyone tape the ceremony?" I smiled, my hands up, hoping it was enough.

"Not your best work. But I think I'm over it. And no, Eric is taking pictures but I don't think they're doing a video. Is that important?"

"To have a record of their wedding? I would think so. Wouldn't you want to...?" And then I regretted changing the topic—the last thing I wanted to discuss was what he wanted at his wedding. At least not until we'd discussed it. And...

Huh...

Yeah, I guess that was how conversations actually happened, wasn't it? And it would be a lot more natural than having the pressure of a sit-down-stare-at-each-other-and-have-the-big-talk conversation.

Maybe the moment could still be salvaged. "We could talk about the future until we land."

He nodded, but before he had a chance to say anything, the plane jerked, and a flight attendant's voice came over the intercom system.

"Ladies and gentlemen, we have just been cleared to land in Fa'a'ā International Airport. Please make sure your seatbelts are securely fastened..." And then more about coming around to pick up trash and make sure we were properly stowed or something.

So much for our coffee and spit. Well, at least I didn't feel as bad for being rude to her.

Then three different voices speaking the three different languages used on the island came on: "*Mesdames et Messieurs, mau Vahine e Homa*, Ladies and Gentlemen. *Bienvenue à Tahiti. Maeva i te Tahiti.* Welcome to Tahiti."

"By the time we get a chance to talk about the future," he said, "it won't be the future anymore."

"And we'll actually be living it, not talking about it."

He turned his body toward me. "This isn't anything official, but I need to know—yes or no." He swallowed. "Do you believe we have a future together?"

"Yes," I said without thinking. "I can't imagine my life without you. But we still have a lot of stuff to work on before—"

"Sorry," he said, his smile stopping my heart for a second. "I quit listening after you said yes. We'll deal with the rest of it later." He faced forward again and let out a long breath, ignoring the fuss of the passengers around us as they gathered their stuff and crowded the aisle. People were pushing up against the curtain dividing first class from coach, as if it were a magical barrier no regular person could cross.

I didn't know what Carson was thinking, but he seemed satisfied to hold my hand in both of his until everyone had filed out of the plane.

"You ready?" he asked after he'd taken our carry-ons from the attendant.

Obviously, he was referring to getting off the airplane but, in that simple statement, I heard so much more.

Was I ready for the next step? Was I ready to commit to forever? Was I ready to try blending two very separate pieces of my life? My past and my future.

He leaned in for a quick kiss. "Come on! If we don't leave now, we might miss the whole 'Bye. Bye! Thanks for flying with us,' line. That's the best part of traveling. But you have to wait until they've said it about seven hundred times and start using different accents to make it less boring. You ready?"

"Yeah. I think I finally am." Saying anything else was unnecessary. For now.

10

CARSON

THE BEST THING about Lane and me was how much we liked each other. Even before the whole love thing happened, there was a ton of like. She was fun and good and got to me in a way no one else ever had before. So it made sense all our recent drama was about the love parts—the expectations, disappointments, and stuff that screwed every couple up—at least all the couples on TV.

Thankfully, as soon as our feet touched the island, all that reality crap disappeared. We fell back into our awesome normal. No bickering, no expectations, no bullshit. Just me making fun of her *oohs* and *ahhs* as we were guided through the hotel lobby, then to our own private hut.

The hut— Fine, most people called them bungalows, but that was a stupid word so I called them huts. Plus it made me feel less like a douche who used words like "bungalow."

Our *hut* was literally beach side and beach-top. Thick wooden posts lifted the floor off the white sand under the translucent, blue-tinted water. As far as the eye could see.

As soon as the valet left us alone, I ripped off my clothes. Unfortunately, Lane said we couldn't start my non-incestuous

Blue Lagoon fantasy until *after* my brother's wedding, so I put on some swim trunks.

"You win this round, babe," I said unhappily. "But there is no way we're not going skinny-dipping while we're here."

"I don't know." She made a face. "Do you have any idea how uncomfortable it is for a woman to get sand in certain parts of her body?"

Huh. Hadn't thought of that. My mind quickly jumped to where I intended a part of *my* body to be spending a lot of time this week.

Sandpaper. On my cock. Fuck no. But I couldn't give up on the dream yet.

"Don't worry, babe. I'll make sure you're clean enough to eat off of. And then you can be as dirty as you want." As long as we were talking about the friction kind of dirty, not the abrasive kind.

Just in case she didn't understand the kind of dirty I was talking about, I took her by the shoulders, gave her a quick kiss, and shoved her onto the bed. Getting her pants off was harder than I would've liked, but I made it happen. I ran a trail of nibbles and licks from her bellybutton to the edge of her panties, my body forcing her legs open.

"Stop, Carson! We can't." Trying not to laugh, she gripped the waistband while I attempted to pull them down. We fought for a little while before I spotted a way in.

"Fine. You win." I lifted my hands up in submission. "I won't take them off."

Then, just as she relaxed her grip, I made my move.

"I'll work around them." One stroke distracted her and made her knees flop open. One more, and my fingers were in the perfect position to get under her panties and pull the fabric to the side. I got down on her before she'd realized what had happened.

Lane protested for about thirty seconds, until my tongue turned her "No, not right now" into "Yes, right there."

As soon as she came, I cursed and dove for my suitcase, pissed I hadn't kept it closer to the bed.

Now, I'm not one of those people who's afraid to eat local cuisine—pun mildly intended—or hesitant to trust the safety of resort diving equipment. The worst thing that could happen would be death. But the one thing I refused to trust in a third-world country were condoms. Because if a condom failed, the result would last for generations. So, I'd packed enough protection to ensure no child was ever conceived on this island again. Population control by Carson Bennett. You're welcome, people of Tahiti.

When Lane saw what took up most of my suitcase, she got off the bed and came closer. "You've got to be kidding. Did you bring any clothes?"

"I don't need clothes." I ripped open a box, pulled them apart, and sprinkled them all over the bed. "I need these." Now I'd have one within reach no matter what position we happened to be in when the time came. Actually, *before* I came. Lane raised an eyebrow when I laughed at my unspoken joke.

"Don't know why, but when you said you'd packed, I assumed you meant clothes." She crossed her arms and stuck out a hip. "Ugh. I'm not going to have to be one of those women who pack for their man, am I?"

"We could always vacation at clothing-optional places. I'm down with that, by the way."

"Too bad I'm not."

"You think I'm fat, don't you?" I patted the six-pack I'd worked hard for. Not at a gym, of course. Nope, this bad boy was the result of a grueling, intensive schedule of fucking Lane in one position or another. And maybe some genetics, I guess.

"Is that really the only reason you can think of for me not wanting to go to those places?"

"Well, what else could it be?" I pressed her body backwards with mine until she had no choice but to climb onto the bed again. And I had no choice but to climb on top of her, pushing condoms away from where I laid her down. "Your body is perfect, especially when you don't have any of those annoying clothes covering it."

"Sure, it is." She wiggled out from under me and scooted farther up on the bed, leaving one leg outstretched. Then she lifted it until her toes were a half-inch away from my face.

"Oh, babe. It is. It so is."

When I bit her—like she deserved—she gasped and tried to jerk her foot away, but I held on. I could feel the vibration of her laugh through her toes, then her ankle, then her knee as I slowly worked my way up her leg, alternating between caress of my lips and brushes of my tongue.

When I looked up, she was propped up on her elbows, holding one of the condoms between her teeth.

I groaned and rested my chin on her knee. "You going to open that?"

She took it out of her mouth and held it up, waving it back and forth. "You mean this?"

Damn, she was sexy, even when she wasn't giving me what I wanted. *Especially* when she wasn't giving me what I wanted.

"I'm not sure," she teased. As I moved up her body, she spread her legs to give me room. "I need to think about it."

"Well, while you're thinking"—I slid one hand behind her neck—"I'll be doing this." I leaned down and lifted her head until our lips met. And met. And then met again, along with our tongues and our hips. Grinding against each other so hard, if we pressed any harder, somebody would've gotten hurt.

Eventually we needed a breather.

Okay, enough breathing for one day. I brushed a lock of her hair off her cheek and dipped my head down to kiss her again.

"Wait," she said, pushing me away playfully. I know she was playing because moving wood and tools around all day had given her some serious upper body strength. Plus she knew where all my most sensitive areas were. And, yes, I'd learned that lesson the hard way.

"Aren't we supposed to meet your family soon?" she asked.

I shook my head. "If I show up on time, they'll get spoiled and start expecting it. They're already spoiled enough and I don't want to enable them anymore."

"Maybe I should try that with you—not enabling you to get into my pants anytime you want to. Wouldn't want to spoil you." She laughed, covering her panties as if I hadn't already gotten around them earlier.

"Spoil me, Lane. Spoil me hard."

"If they're mad, I'm blaming you."

"It'll be worth it."

The huts were about thirty feet apart but I would have to ask how well sound traveled over water to know how soundproof they were. Unfortunately for them, our neighbors were going to hear all about how she'd spoiled me for all others.

11

CARSON

As I happily drifted off into post-hurrah bliss, Lane rolled off me and went over to a shower stall made entirely out of glass. Someday I'd have to track down the architect who designed this place and thank him.

I ogled her as she soaped herself up. The only thing that would make this better would be if she started dancing.

"We were supposed to meet everyone fifteen minutes ago." Before her hands reached her breasts, she stopped and looked at me. "So stop gawking at me like a pervert and get in here..." She laughed. "Like a pervert."

I'd follow directions like that any time. I stepped into the waterfall of warm water and slipped my arms around her from the back.

She turned toward me and started washing my chest. "Everyone's meeting in the bar."

"Says who?"

"Clare emailed the weekend's itinerary to everyone. Didn't you read it?"

"Nope." Not only did I never check my email, but I never, *ever* checked my email for messages from my family.

Even though Clare was no longer married to my older brother, she hadn't divorced my family for some reason, so she still counted.

"The last thing I want is written proof I'm going to be forced to spend time with my family. It's less painful to make it a surprise—less pre-event anxiety and more in-the-moment adrenaline."

"Makes perfect sense." She pushed me back a step so she could rinse off. Then, trying to avoid any soap transfer from me to her, she squeezed against the glass wall to get past me and left me to rinse myself.

After drying off, she slipped a thin blue dress over her head. "Don't you think it's weird Hayden's ex-wife is planning a wedding for him and his *next* wife?"

"You should know by now, everything about my family is weird. Weird or tragic." It should have been engraved on the Bennett crest.

I didn't say anything more until I'd turned the water off and stepped out from behind the glass. "For instance, my brother actually invited Renee and Anna here. If that's not tragic, I don't know what is."

"It's tragic that Hayden wants your mother and your step-sister at his wedding?"

"It's bad juju. Renee and Anna are each walking bad luck charms for relationships, so having both of them? In one place? At the same time? Honestly, I won't be surprised if this island sinks into the ocean tonight. We should wear masks and snorkels to bed."

"You're too hard on them. Yes, your mom and stepsister have...*questionable* taste in relationships."

"Nope. No question about it. It's horrific."

"But Hayden and Andi also invited Andi's friends, two of

whom have been happily married to each other for four years or so."

"Emilia and Rob? Sure, they're alright. Or they hide their dysfunction well."

"Hillary and Eric will get here tomorrow—they're happy."

"He's only here to photograph the wedding, and Hillary's pretending to be his assistant so she can tag along. Nope, they don't count."

She sighed, sticking one hip out and crossing her arms. "*We're* here. Are you going to tell me we don't count either?"

"Hmmm..." I hung my towel over a hook, grabbed her arm, and yanked her into me. "You have a point. But, just in case, we're going to have to work overtime on the lovin' parts to create enough good juju to counteract their bad mojo."

"For the sake of Hayden's and Andi's future happiness, of course."

"Obviously. Why else would we do it?"

"Get dressed." She pulled away from me and tossed me a t-shirt. "I promised them we'd be there."

"And I promised myself we'd use all these condoms before going home. I allocated a certain number for each day, and we can't fall behind." I shrugged. "One of us is going to have to break their promise, Lane. Guess what my priority is."

"There's another option."

"If you're about to suggest we split up—you go hang out with my family and I stay here alone with the condoms—I *definitely* vote no."

"How about we go meet your family now...?"

I waited. Impatiently and not particularly excitedly. Whatever idea she came up with would be a step down from what I wanted.

"And then, when we come back here tonight, we stay up as long as it takes to make up for the time we missed."

My cock instantly perked up and listened. Lane's sex drive was never lacking, but it had been a while since we did a marathon. "What if it takes all night?"

"I said, 'As long as it takes,' Carson."

I pretended to consider the idea, weigh all the options. "All in favor say, 'Fuck, yeah.'"

"Fuck, yeah," we said simultaneously.

She laughed as we left the hut and walked over the wooden dock that led to dry land. "I love how well our voices go together."

"Me too." I took her hand and pulled her closer to me. "Almost as much as I love how well *we* go together."

When she looked up at me and *ahhed*, I realized she thought I was being romantic. Got to break those expectations before they had a chance to take hold.

So I added, "Which will be happening repeatedly tonight."

"Why do I feel like you made a big deal about your family just to get what you'd been hoping for all along?"

I shrugged. "No idea. Hope and my family are two things that have never entered my mind at the same time."

We accidentally met Anna in the hotel lobby. She looked great —no surprise there. Looking great was one of the things Anna did best. She came up to us, smiling. After my shivers passed, I acknowledged her with a nod.

She and I had come a long way in our relationship, but I knew better than to trust her again or forgive her. She was too good at hurting the people she cared about most. Maybe someday that would change, but she still had a lot of proving herself to do.

She hugged Lane with one of those society, don't-actually-touch-the-person-you're-hugging hugs. She didn't bother trying to touch, or pretend to touch, me.

"Isn't this place gorgeous?" Lane asked, gesturing around us. The lobby was open-air so guests could enjoy the view of the water while they checked in or had a drink.

"Absolutely. My only complaint is I wish I'd thought to bring a date. I'm going to be the only one without someone."

"I'm sure you'll find a stand-in," I said. "In fact, I'm surprised you haven't already found someone unsuitable. There's gotta be at least a couple men in the bar whose wives have gone back to their rooms for a nap. That's usually how you find them, isn't it?"

Both women stared at me as if I weren't speaking the truth. If there was an unavailable man within thirty yards, Anna would find him. Especially if he was also an asshole who would treat her like shit.

"Ah, crap, sis. Aren't you feeling well?"

She glared at me briefly. "I'm feeling fine. Thanks for asking, Carson. You're always such a gentleman."

"Only where you're concerned. Promise."

Lane put her hand on my arm and squeezed, letting me know I should behave myself.

Right. Deep breath. Keep my rude but true comments to myself.

This trip was about my brother and his bride-to-be's happiness. Therefore, no one else's happiness or comfort mattered. Good thing being around Anna or Renee didn't naturally supply any of that.

"Andi made reservations at a restaurant at the south end of the island," Anna said. "I have no idea how big this island actually is, but I hope we won't have to walk there."

"Me too." Lane stuck out her foot. "I'm not used to walking in heels."

When Anna's brow constricted, I figured out two things:

One, her preventative Botox injections had worn off, and two, she really couldn't comprehend why a woman would *choose* to wear flat shoes. The only shoes I'd ever seen her in were heels a good couple inches higher than Lane's new ones.

Ever the unwilling gentleman, I let Anna take my other arm as we walked into the bar area just off the lobby. Andi's whole crew was at the opposite end, sitting around a table with fruity drinks in front of them and laughing. Even Hayden had something pink in his glass. He dropped the little umbrella into it when he saw us.

"Hey, family!" he called, standing and kissing Lane and Anna hello before pulling a few more chairs over. I helped him, waiting until the ladies had seats before circling the table for the individual hello-good-to-see-you-again thing.

The group had subconsciously divided by parties—Andi and Hayden obviously sat next to each other, but her friends Emilia, Rob, and Sara sat on her side, while Lane, Anna, and I sat on Hayden's. To my knowledge, the only other people who'd gotten invitations and plane tickets to the wedding were my mother—because Hayden felt a familial obligation I didn't—and Hayden's ex-wife, Clare.

"What do you guys want to drink?" Andi asked.

"I'm dying to try whatever Hayden was drinking," I said, laughing at him.

"She forced me to," he grumbled. "I made her a promise—one girlie drink."

"It's true," Andi said. "He's a man of his word. Now that he's fulfilled his obligation, I'm guessing he'll never order one again."

Hayden shrugged. "I'm also a man who has found pleasure in doing the unexpected."

She looked confused, everyone smiled, and I laughed out loud until everyone looked at me, including Hayden. I wasn't going to tattle on him. He'd told me all about his kickass surprise gift for her before making the final walk-through *my* problem.

When Hay had been born, all my parents' responsible genes had gone into him, leaving none for me. Every plan I'd come up with had ended with Lane unhappy or in pain—and not the good kind.

"What?" I asked. "It's a brother thing." It wasn't. Or maybe it was. I kind of liked our new relationship, one where neither of us would break into a rash when we admitted we were head-over-heels, goofy in love with our women.

"Speaking of... Let's go talk about brotherhood, Carson." Hayden gave Andi a quick smooch and then stood, hinting with his eyes that I do the same. I thought about pretending to misunderstand him and leaning over to kiss Andi too. But that would've freaked out everyone at the table and, considering the potential for conflict Lane and I had been experiencing lately, I decided the joke wasn't worth making. So I kissed my girlfriend —not his—and followed him away from the table.

As soon as the bar was between us and the table, he turned his back on the group and whispered, "Is *it* all set up on your end?"

Was it all set up on my end? Since when were we in an old spy film?

"Be careful. Any one of them might be able to read lips," I whispered back, holding my hand directly in front of my mouth and laughing. "Don't worry, bro. I did exactly what I was supposed to do, in exactly the way you demanded I do it."

"It's important, Carson."

"Shit, Hay. I know it's important. And I'm not being sarcastic. Well, only partially sarcastic. But it's all taken care of. Your whole house is now smarter than both of us combined."

"That's not saying much," he mumbled. "Did you bring video like I asked?"

"You mean ordered? Yes, sir, I did." I pulled out my phone, found the video clips Sean had sent, and handed the phone to him. He quietly watched the walk-through of the house, and I nodded along with Sean's narration as if I knew how any of that shit worked. On video, Sean explained everything he'd added—solar panels, lights, temperature, music, security, sprinklers, kitchen appliances, showers, and door locks that could be controlled by an app, the remote, or vocal recognition. Basically, every automated bell and whistle a techno-freak like Andi could ever dream of.

I had to give it to my brother—he knew his woman well. She'd techno-freak *out* as soon as she saw it.

"Hayden? Just thinking out loud here—"

"Do you ever think *silently*?" he shot back.

"Never. Why keep all of my wisdom from the rest of the world?" I quickly added, "That was rhetorical."

"Too bad."

"Anyway, here's my concern: The remote symbolizes a man's last shred of control in a relationship. Handing it over to your woman leaves you completely powerless. Is that really what you want, brother? To be powerless?

"Plus, have you considered the possibility she'll love playing with the new gadgets so much, she might forget you're even there?"

"Sure. I've also considered the fact that, if the toilet seat automatically lowers and the refrigerator reminds me to pick up milk on the way home, we'll have less to fight about as a married couple."

Wow. "I take it back—you're *almost* as smart as your house."

"She'll like it, right?"

Hayden was decisive and stubborn as hell. Every decision was made and stuck to. The end. I'd never seen him second guess himself like this. Not to mention he'd never needed my assurance before. I kind of liked it.

"She'll *love* it, bro. She'll get all gushy and blushy about it." I slapped him on the back. "Honestly, I don't get why you have to buy her a present at all. Isn't handing over our eternity enough for women nowadays? In the olden days, we menfolk got all the gifts—pigs and goats and shit for the home front, right?"

"Like a dowry?" he asked, looking at me skeptically. "Yep, men sure had it good back then. Pigs and goats...and disease, an average lifespan of thirty-five years, no showers, and no birth control. The last one wouldn't matter, of course, because you couldn't sleep with your bride until after you were married and even then, she'd probably been taught it was her wifely duty to just lie there and take it. So that must've been lots of fun."

"Hmm...I take back every criticism I've ever made about the modern-day world."

"Great. I'm glad I know you're so dowry driven. So now, if you ever propose to Laney, I'll be sure to let her know you've always wanted a baby pig that fits in your purse."

"No need. She's already got a pig"—I slapped myself in the chest—"right here."

"I'm so happy for you both." He didn't look happy. He looked like he wondered if Lane would ever marry so far beneath her. "Speaking of you being happy, have you seen our mother yet?"

"Damn it, she's here? I was hoping her plane would go down." I glanced around the bar, still hoping. "When did she get here?"

"Two days ago, but she's been touring the island, trying to stay out of the way."

"Sounds like Renee." Always staying out of the way unless she wanted something from you.

Maybe that wasn't fair. Maybe, now that she was trying to get her shit together, was avoiding men who would hit her, and hadn't married someone in two whole years, I should have given her more credit. Thing was, I'd played along with her bullshit, pretended to be the dutiful son, and had covered the bruises left by my father and every other man she loved, ever since she'd taught me how to lie. So, no matter how sorry she was or how much I wanted to forgive her, I figured she still had about nineteen more years of crap to make up for.

But this weekend wasn't about me or Renee. It was about Hayden, Andi, love, and skinny dipping.

I focused on the last one to make me smile. "Where's Clare? I thought she'd be at the entrance to the bar, checking boxes next to our names and telling us where to sit, what to drink, and when we were allowed to take a sip."

"Believe me, I'm sure she would be if she wasn't already too busy screaming at the hotel staff about something." Hayden shrugged and rolled his eyes. "She was so unhappy about *our* wedding, she never really got into it. This is her chance to plan the hell out of one, and after everything she's gone through, I think she deserves it. As long as she doesn't anger the staff too much..."

"Oh please." I laughed. "I bet you a hundred bucks you've already apologized and tipped them all enough to deal with anything Clare throws at them—literally *and* figuratively."

His brow lifted and he suddenly looked like he'd gotten too much sun. "You won't tell her, will you?"

"Tell someone how damn nice my brother is? Definitely not. I already wonder if Lane is with me just to get close to my perfect older brother."

I couldn't exactly judge Hayden and Clare's very mature and amicable post-relationship relationship and his decision to invite his ex-wife to his wedding. Especially because if—*when*—Lane and I ever tied the noose—I mean, *knot*—she'd want Hillary there.

Unfortunately, Hillary and I had gotten together once, way before I met Lane, but there was nothing mature or amicable about our relationship. Thankfully, our better halves had moved past it. Primarily because we were in much better places now than we'd been then.

All of us were. Huh. I wouldn't think that was too common. Actually, until I'd met Lane and Hayden had met Andi, I wouldn't have thought that was even *possible*.

12

CARSON

EVERY SINGLE PERSON I knew was happier and *hopier* than they'd been a couple years ago. Well, I'm sure *someone* was miserable now. Someone was always miserable. It usually didn't take more than a quick glance to see who was crap at hiding their true feelings.

Ironically, when I looked back at the table, the first person I saw was Anna. See? Someone was always miserable, whether self-induced or not. My wicked stepsister was leaning back in the teak chair, one long, tanned leg crossed over the other as if she were meant to own the world. Hell, maybe she was.

Of course, she had a lot of twelve-step programs to go through before that had a chance of happening.

Across the table, Andi and Emilia were laughing about something Rob had said. Andi's other friend, Sara, was looking out at the water, pushing her thoughts out to sea, maybe.

Obviously, I saved the best for last. When Lane caught me looking, her smile appeared, but it hadn't been there a second before.

"Is everything alright with Laney?" Hayden must have seen the same thing I did. "It seems like something's bothering her."

I could've just given the jet lag excuse, but I knew he wouldn't buy it. At least not as the only reason. "We had a minor hiccup before we left San Francisco. Nothing terrible, but it's lingering."

"Make sure you fix it before the ceremony. If Andi thinks there's something wrong, she might worry about it. I don't want anything to ruin this for her."

"Promise." I put up my right hand and pantomimed putting my left on a bible. "We'll be fine. I think we just need some one-on-one time. The less fun kind."

"I told you not to blow this, Carson. In fact, I believe my exact words were, 'Move fast, before Laney realizes what a screw-up you are.'"

"Wow, with big-bro advice like that, I'm not sure why I ever fantasize about strangling you."

"I thought I was the only one who did that." He smacked me on the back. "I only want the best for you, Carson. And Laney is definitely best for you. But sometimes I worry your self-destructive half will take over and ruin the one good thing you have."

Me, too. "Heredity is tough to overcome, you know?" Sometimes, I can almost feel those genes pushing against my rational, sane mind, making me want to pick a fight I knew how to win. So far, with the exception of the other night, I'd been able to control it. But it was still in me, looking for a chance to take over and bring down everything good Lane and I had built.

"You're stronger than you know, little brother. So is Laney. One thing Andi has taught me is that life is meant to be lived, not endured. And when you find the person you're supposed to be with, the strength of both of you combined can overcome any personal defects either of you possess. Lucky for you, you're a Bennett, which means those defects are blatantly obvious to everyone. So the trick is finding someone who's brave enough to point them out to you."

I nodded, in total agreement. A lifetime of living one way, believing you were incapable of love, and then finding out you were completely wrong, wasn't easy. In the past year, I'd had to unlearn everything I'd ever been taught.

"Can I ask you something?" I said, just as he turned to go back to the table.

"Sure. Unless it's about my sex life...or yours." At least he was smiling as he said it.

"So... I'm thinking of...um..." I took a deep breath. Shit, if I couldn't say it to my brother, how was I ever supposed to say it to Lane? "So Lane and I have been together for a while. And, in her family and some others evidently, marriage isn't always tragic. And, you know, you're getting married..."

"Yes, Carson, I know." He watched my discomfort for another minute or so. "You're finally going to ask Laney to marry you."

I kind of grunted, which was all I could do to admit it.

"Hallelujah," he said, his smile huge. "When and how can I help?"

"Um...I don't know and you can't...I don't think."

"Just to be clear though, we *are* talking about marriage, right?"

I took another, deeper breath before nodding, as if a head bob was a lifelong commitment in and of itself.

He walked me a little farther down the bar, held onto my shoulders, and looked into my eyes. "Little brother, you do understand you're going to have to say it out loud, don't you? I suppose you could do it in a note, but I think most women prefer to know their prospective life partners are able to speak to them without going into anaphylactic shock."

"I talk to her all the time. Just not about..."

"Marriage. Say it."

"Marriage." I threw up my hands. "See? I can say it."

"Impressive. Now, let's try something harder." He spoke slowly. "Will you marry me?"

I stared at him for a sec. "Oh, man. This is awkward." I should let him off easy. "I like you. I really do. But see... Well, for starters, we're brothers. And even though the same-sex marriage thing was figured out, I don't think the brother thing will ever be legal. Second, you're already getting married so, again, not legal. At least not in California. But the third and most important thing is I'm in love with someone else."

"It's probably for the best." Feigning disappointment, Hayden shook his head at me while calling the bartender over to us. "I understand alcohol is a good way to get over life's greatest disappointments. Want one?"

He knew me well enough not to wait for an answer, ordering two bottles of Hinano and three bottles of Champagne to be sent over to the table. All while I pondered how to explain my anxiety over the word. As soon as the bartender put the beer in front of me, I slammed it back, the cold liquid forcing its way past the tightness of my throat and landing happily in my gut.

"Marriage can be a good thing, right?" I set the half-empty bottle down and signaled for another.

"Of course. Marriage is a promise. A commitment. Telling the world you intend to stay with this person for the rest of your life, carry them when they need to be carried and accept their help when *you* need to be carried."

"Romantic, bro."

As soon as he turned to face me straight on and put his hand on my shoulder, I knew I was in for some tough brotherly love. Unfortunately I couldn't think of an excuse to leave before it started. Plus I didn't have my second beer yet.

"Here's what you need to ask yourself, little brother. Number one: Do you love Laney?"

Truthfully? No. People could fall out of love, and I'd never fall out of whatever this was. So *love* was too weak a word for what I felt for her.

"Number two: Can you imagine your life without her?"

Yes. But it would be miserable and pointless and not one I'd want to live.

"Number three: Do you want to grow old with her?"

Yes *and* no. I hoped we'd have years and years and years together. But if it were up to me, she'd live forever, be there for our kids and grandkids and everyone she came in contact with. Whether I was there or not.

"Those are bullshit questions, bro." I emptied my first beer and handed it to the bartender just as he set down the new one. "A teenager could figure out which answer you wanted."

His smile was slow to form. "Thankfully, you're not a teenager anymore, Carson. You're a man." He cocked his head. "Most of the time. And, while anyone can answer the questions, only a man can decide if he's answering them truthfully. Only a man can decide to become the person he needs to be so that the woman he loves will never doubt his answers."

My drink stopped halfway to my mouth, my mind stuck somewhere between "You don't know what you're talking about," and "I should probably be sober when I admit how right you are."

Fuck it, admitting it would be *easier* if I were drunk. Said, slurred—what was the difference? But you should never drink alone. So, when Hay started to walk back to the group, I ordered a round of shots for everyone, an extra for me, and a pink slushy drink with an umbrella in it for Hayden.

13

CARSON

ONE THING I'd always been good at was knowing how to leave a party right before the fight broke out, especially this one. Hint: My mother arrived.

Renee walked into the bar as if it were hers, as if the entire island was created at her bidding. I stood there silently and watched her welcome the group to *her* island like she was Mr. Roarke from a bad remake of *Fantasy Island.*

Smiles, everyone! Smiles! And air-kisses all around!

Yep. Time to leave. Hayden hurried back to the table. I took it a little slower so I...didn't spill my beer. Right.

When my unexcited steps brought me back to the table, I accepted Renee's brief and fairly cold hug. Didn't even have to put down my drinks. I mean, yes, she and I had a moment of understanding a while ago, and yes, she was trying to be more human, but she still had a long way to go.

When she took someone else's seat right next to Andi, I leaned closer to my brother and whispered, "The longer I'm around her, the more likely you'll have to find a new best man, one who *hasn't* been arrested. So can Lane and I be excused, please?"

He sighed, nodded solemnly, and went to take the seat on his fiancée's other side.

I grabbed Lane. "Sorry, everyone. We won't be able to do dinner because we need to go...somewhere else. But we'll definitely see you all later."

Lane looked at me with disappointed understanding. As soon as we were out of earshot, she asked, "Are you going to be able to make it through an entire weekend?"

"As long as I pace myself. And by *pace*, I mean lots of sex breaks and time on the beach. Or a combination of the two."

"How about we start with the beach and see what happens?"

I could handle that. The sun wouldn't set for another couple of hours. Plenty of time to get her horny and not *enough* time for her to get so sunburnt she wouldn't let me touch her.

The resort's private beach was a little less secluded than I would have liked, but it was practically empty. Mostly because the resort was so exclusive, we'd just left a quarter of the guests in the bar talking.

Only one other group was enjoying the sun, a family of three. Mom and Dad seemed to have had lots and lots of practice ignoring each other. High quality apathy over there. And their kid? Yeah, I recognized the look on his face. Puberty had just grabbed him by the balls, and all he wanted to do was go *home* and be neglected there, like normal. At least he'd have his computer, online porn, and a door he could lock there. I'd worn that look a lot growing up.

"I could get used to this." Laney stretched out on the beach blanket, her legs freshly slathered with sunscreen by yours truly. It was a tough job, especially on her upper thighs, but...

"Me, too." I crawled around behind her to get her back and

sides, and as much of her breasts as I could before she swatted my hands away. "Seeing you covered in my cream..."

"Ugh. There's a teenager over there, Carson." She grabbed the sunscreen from me and scooted away. "I think you've had about enough of that."

"Not even close, babe." I reached for her, swiping at air as she moved out of fondling distance.

"Let's go for a walk." She stood, brushed off her ass, and held out her hand to pull me up. Since it was for resort guests only, and most of them kept their thieving exclusively for their businesses at home, we didn't have to worry about our stuff.

We held hands as we walked into the water, just deep enough to get our ankles wet. The ocean was fucking gorgeous here, but the water was so warm, it didn't feel like a break from the sun. In fact, it was so close to body temperature, and the waves were so tiny, it felt pretty much like our bathtub at home. Other than the people watching us here. Hmm...wonder if Lane would be up to trying that when we got back.

Lane pulled me deeper until the water was about waist-high. She slipped her hands around my neck and jumped into my arms. I gratefully caught her under her ass, and she wrapped her legs around me.

"Am I too heavy?"

"Not at all. But if a shark comes along, you know I'm going to drop you and run for it, right?"

"Of course," she said, smiling. "No problem—I can handle a shark."

"What if it's a *big* shark?"

"Depends who's measuring." Laughing, she ground her hips on mine, and my big shark woke right up. "Men always seem to think things are larger than they actually are."

"You've never complained before."

"I complain all the time, just not about that."

"I've never heard you complain. You must be doing it wrong. Try whining more next time so I know."

"Like this?" she asked in a high, nasal voice, her nose and upper lip rising and making her look as close to unattractive as possible.

"That'd do it." I tried kissing her, but with her mouth contorted like that, I got more teeth than lip. Pina Colada-flavored.

She pulled away. "What were you talking to your brother about at the bar earlier?"

"Do you always think about my brother while we're kissing?"

"Jealous?" she asked. The brat. "Or do you just not want to answer the question?"

"Always, and no. I'd rather make out than talk about Hayden."

"Then answer quick so we can get back to it."

I sighed. "Fine." I spoke faster than an auctioneer on speed. "He planned a surprise wedding gift for Andi back home. I'm helping him with it." Done speaking, I leaned in for my prize.

"Really?" Pulling away, she did that girlie inhalation that lifted her breasts up beautifully, as well as her brow and the corners of her mouth. Like she was the world's most perfect marionette or something. "How romantic! What is it?"

I shook my head. "If I tell you, it won't be a surprise." I would've zipped my lips if my hands weren't happy where they were—cupping her ass so nicely. Good thing the water was deep enough to cover us or the thirteen-year-old kid staring at us from shore would've gotten quite a show.

"The surprise is for Andi, not me. So spill."

As much as I liked to tease her, she'd find out eventually. "Promise you won't say anything."

"I promise."

"Promise me that if you break said promise, you will let me

do every deviant thing I can imagine to you while saying, 'Please, sir, may I have some more?' Complete with the English accent."

She stared at me for a minute, stunned or maybe trying to figure out what deviant thing I could be referring to that we hadn't already tried.

"Promise," she said finally, in an English accent.

"That's my girl." I kind of hoped she told someone. Then I could spank her. Screw it, I was going to spank her whether she told anyone or not.

"It really worries me when you laugh like that."

Oops. "Okay but remember your promise—no blabbing to the girls."

"Is that the only thing you think women do when there are no men around? *Talk* about the men who aren't around?"

"Of course, not. You also do your nails, practice kissing, and have pillow fights. At least that's what I'd like to *think* you're doing. Okay, tell you what, you don't ruin my fantasy, and I'll tell you what Hayden is giving Andi for a wedding gift."

"Deal," she said, rolling her eyes. "By the way, we also discuss orgasms."

"Awesome." I could definitely work that into my fantasy. She nudged me when I got so lost in my daydream I forgot my end of the deal. "Right. Hayden is smartening up their place. *Smartening*, meaning adding a thousand gadgets that automatically do shit for you, not *smartening up the place* like cleaning and adding a couple throw pillows. Andi will be able to dim the lights, heat up the bed, and put on music to set the mood without lifting a finger."

Her jaw dropped as I spoke and excitement filled her eyes. "I've heard of that stuff. It's so cool! Did they get the fridge that will tell you if you're out of comfort food without you having to open the door?"

I nodded. "Warming toilet seat, shower that's programmed to be the perfect temperature and vacuuming robot thing, too. Basically, everything the Jetsons had, except the flying car. I think he's saving that for their five-year anniversary."

"Wow." She took a deep breath of longing. "That's the sweetest thing I've ever heard of."

"Yeah? If you want a smart house, we can smarten up our place."

"It'd be cool, but that's not the point. It's perfect because Hayden is creating a home just for them. He's taking something Andi already loves—the house she grew up in—and making it even better by adding something else she loves—technology. If it was for anyone else, the gadgets would be cool and fun, but for Andi, it'll be a constant reminder of how well her husband understands her. That's why it's perfect. Do you know what I mean?"

"No. Maybe after we get back to the city, I can ask Hayden and Andi's smart house to explain it to me."

Actually, I did understand. I just wished I didn't. Because now I had proof I needed to come up with something equally amazing for her. No, *more* amazing for her. Damn it. The longer I waited to make things official, the more potential pitfalls showed up. What would be *perfect* to her? I couldn't wait anymore. I had to figure this out.

Now.

14

CARSON

"LANE." I took a deep breath and set her down, the water coming up to just under her breasts. "I want to ask you about something."

"Sounds serious," she said, making a face and mocking my sudden change in mood.

"It is...kind of."

I wasn't going to pop any questions, but if I could get some info out of her—something that might give me a clue as to what her perfect proposal and ideal aftermath were—it would be really helpful.

Or maybe a "Yes, Carson, I absolutely, definitely, 100 percent want to spend the rest of my life with you, starting with a huge wedding with 10,000 people we don't know or care about. I'll wear white"—then I'd make a bad joke—"and you can wear jeans. We'll honeymoon in Las Vegas for a month and have sex a couple times a day for the rest of our lives, even after all our little munchkins are born! But, whatever you do, please, please, please, don't propose in a memorable or creative way. I'd rather you just slip the ring under my coffee cup and forget all that romantic crap."

"Why are you smiling like that?" she asked, one eyebrow raised.

"No reason. It's just... I hope you know how much I love you."

"I do." As soon as the words left her mouth, she gasped. "I didn't mean—"

"What?" I asked, pretending not to know why she was embarrassed. I had to start over. "What I was going to ask you is—"

When her face registered scared shock, I shut my mouth. Shit, I hadn't even asked her anything yet. But she must have known I planned to. So did that look mean she was going to say no?

"Carson!" She screamed and jumped back into my arms, clutching me tightly.

Was that a yes? Hang on. I wasn't sure I knew what the hell was actually happening right now. She kept spinning her head around, looking for something. Plus, you know, she hadn't stopped screaming.

"What did I miss?"

"Something just bit me!"

"What?" Oh shit. What I'd assumed was shock had actually been pain.

"Get me out of here!"

I moved fast, pulling her tightly to me and heading for shore, just like we wished people in horror movies would do instead of standing there wondering what to do. I fought the water, praying I didn't lose my footing or feel jaws close around my ass. *Get her to the beach.* Whatever happened to me, I just needed to make sure she was safe.

Couldn't have been more than ten seconds before we reached the shore, but the journey had wiped me out. I tripped on sand, catching the bulk of my bodyweight before it landed full force on top of her. Then I heard her giggle.

I pushed myself onto both hands and stared down at her. Laughing.

Both of us were gasping for breath, me because I couldn't get the newspaper headline out of my mind—*Man Eaten by Shark Ruins Brother's Wedding*—and Lane because she couldn't stop laughing.

"Oh, Carson, you should've seen your face!"

Why? I could imagine pretty damn well how stupid I'd looked already.

"Did something bite you or not?" I asked, still confused or in shock or confused or something. Or possibly confused.

She nodded quickly. "But I'm okay. More scared-the-shit-out-of-me than took-a-chunk-out-of-me." Then her expression softened to concern. "I'm sorry! I totally freaked you out, didn't I?"

"Course not," I lied. I couldn't really tell her why I'd looked that way or how she'd turned a potentially memorable moment into a terrifyingly memorable one. Although, either way... "Let me see this horrible injury of yours. Damned fish better not have ruined your ass."

"It's actually really starting to hurt." Grimacing, she rolled out from under me, onto her stomach, and pulled her bikini bottom off one cheek. "Is it swollen?"

"Yep. As perfectly swollen as always. Still the only reason I'm with you. Other than your breasts. And you're—"

"Carson!" she snapped. "Can you see any teeth marks or anything?"

"I could, if you'd ever let me bite you, but no, babe. There's a little red mark, though. Like if you'd ever let me spank you."

"Stop it! It's not funny."

"Are you okay?" a voice said from a few feet away. It was the thirteen-year-old, and he was staring at my girlfriend's bare ass.

"She's fine. Go away." I tried to block the kid's spank-worthy view.

"It could've been a jellyfish sting. Some of them are poisonous here. Maybe she got poisoned."

Each time he said the P-word, Lane flinched. "What kind of poison are we talking about?"

I held up my hand to shut him up before he started a detailed rundown of every type of murderous sea creature he'd seen on Animal Planet, in the order of how painful a death they caused.

"You gotta learn how to talk to women, little man," I mumbled. "It wasn't a jellyfish." I didn't think. "If it were, I'd have gotten stung too because my hands were all over your..." I glared at the kid. "Your upper, upper leg."

If the little shit weren't standing right next to us, I'd offer to suck out the poison just on the off chance it *was* a jellyfish. At least being angry at me for joking around would distract Lane from the pain.

"But we should probably... Holy—" I swear, a huge welt grew in front of my eyes, a thin line of ass-flesh swelling up and turning from pink to eww.

"What?" she yelled. "Carson, what's wrong?"

"Nothing, babe. Nothing. You're fine." With a fake smile and a pounding heart, I swept her up into my arms and carried her toward the resort's front desk, hoping they had a surgeon on staff.

Turned out the kid was right. Some jellyfish in this part of the world *were* poisonous. I also learned that the pain of their stings got worse after the initial shock wore off. After twenty minutes of ice, the staff doctor put some goop on it, told me to continue putting goop on it until the goop-tube was empty, and gave Lane a couple pills and more ice.

"You'll be sore for a few days, but the pain will dissipate soon."

"Will she ever be able to use it again, doc?"

They both stared at me in shock.

"I meant to sit down!" I lied. "Geez!"

"I can handle it no matter how much it hurts," Lane told the doctor while still looking at me. "Especially considering I *live* with a bigger pain in the ass."

"Who?" I asked as innocently as I could manage.

15

LANEY

THE NEXT MORNING, I watched the sun come up, its light catching on waves so tiny I could barely see them. My butt felt a little better today, but it had kept me up most of the night. Carson had tried to stay up, listen to me complain, and put more of the cream on the sting. Surprisingly, he only quoted *Silence of the Lambs* once. "It puts the lotion in the basket." Thankfully my glare had conveyed the threat perfectly: "Say it again and I'll be off this island and back in the states before they find your body."

He got up when someone from the hotel came out to our bungalow with a breakfast feast. Seriously, the spread was ridiculous—twenty different kinds of pastries, two full carafes of juice, a small mountain of weird kinds of fruit, soft-boiled eggs in cute little shot glass-looking things, and of course, coffee. The next time I saw the man, I promised myself to make sure all the leftovers were given away. If not, I'd have to sit there—figuratively speaking because *ouch*—all day and eat all of it. Not because I wanted to, but because my parents would disown me if I ever wasted this much food while there were starving people in the world.

This island was so beautiful, I could barely sit still. Granted, part of that might have been because it took me five minutes to sit down and every move after that caused me to silently scream, grab whatever part of Carson was closest, and squeeze until his pain was somewhat comparable to mine. It wasn't fair he could sit down like a normal person.

Not sure why I was surprised. *Of course,* I'd get stung by a jellyfish on my first trip outside the country. My first big vacation with Carson and I couldn't sit down without wincing. Yep, that was how my life worked. But now wasn't the time to dwell on my butt or my disappointment. Now was the time to celebrate this moment with Hayden and Andi.

After breakfast, Carson and I got dressed in regular clothes but brought our clothes for the wedding with us. The plan was for the women to meet in Andi's room to help each other and have some girl time. The men—Hayden, Carson, and Rob—would be in another room waiting for us to get ready. Knowing how impatient Carson was, I'd put money on the mini bar and possibly the hotel bar being empty by the time the wedding started.

I didn't expect to see Renee and Anna until the afternoon. Carson told me they planned to spend the day getting rubbed down, squeezed, lifted, injected, waxed, polished, peeled, and slathered with enough toxins to guarantee they'd look pre-pubescent again.

The only way Eric and Hillary could afford the trip was by not paying for it at all. Instead, Carson had hired them to take pictures of the wedding as part of his gift to Hayden and Andi. He'd paid for their plane tickets and a hotel room that cost more than Eric had made in his entire photographic career. He'd even let Eric take credit for it, as reparations for the unfortunate three-hour mistake Carson had made with Hillary long before we'd met.

Before Carson and I split up to report to our designated

gender-zones, he kissed me. When he instinctually slid his hand from my lower back down to my butt where the sting was, he was lucky I only shoved him backwards. I could've grabbed whatever part of him was closest and squeezed. And the part I would've grabbed happened to be his favorite.

The beach, the hotel, and the bungalows were all right out of a dream. Thankfully the bridal suite was bigger than most apartments in San Francisco. There was plenty of room for our little party.

Andi—the nervous bride-to-be; Emilia—Andi's happily married, boss-slash-matron-of-honor; Sara—the distracted-and-possibly-drunk bridesmaid; and Clare—the completely panicked wedding planner-slash-ex-wife of the groom-to-be. Oh, and me, the unmarried, confused chick who couldn't even drink her cares away because she was taking pain medication for her sore ass.

"I'm going to leave you in the...capable hands of your wedding party." Clare smiled at me, but I'd heard the pause in her comment, as well as the panicked look on her face. Yeah, capable. Sure. "I just want to double-check—"

"Quadruple-check," someone muttered.

"—with Eric to make sure he's set up in the right spot."

"Say hi to Hillary for me," I said as Clare rushed toward the door. I hadn't seen Eric or Hillary since they'd arrived this morning. Clare had made my bestie her unofficial assistant whenever Hillary wasn't assisting her photographer boyfriend. Or *fiancé*, I should call him now. Geez, it was hard to keep up.

"You look beautiful, Andi," Clare yelled as the door shut.

"She's right," Emilia said. "You do. And to think you'd planned to hide this gorgeousness behind a computer screen for the rest of your days."

"And I would've gotten away with it, too," Andi said, smiling. "If it hadn't been for you meddling kids."

Yep, everything was perfect, including the bride. Andi looked stunning, her hair swept up in the twist I'd already spent a good half hour fighting for. I was shocked she still had hair, I was yanking on it so hard. The other two women had given up, probably because they knew exactly what that hair was and wasn't capable of—a lesson I'd learned after only a few minutes. But by then, I had something to prove. Plus, Andi and I were about to be family...kind of. Almost? Well, she was about to become a member of a family I hoped to someday be a part of, even if that meant I'd have to occasionally spend time with the *other* members of the family, Anna and Renee.

Thankfully they weren't here with us right now, so I could enjoy my almost-family without any drama. Other than the drama of Andi's hair.

"Now I understand why you always wear it in a ponytail," I said as I jammed a few more bobby pins in it.

"Back off, Laney!" Andi snapped. When she saw me flinch, she gasped and clenched her eyes shut. "I'm so sorry. That totally came out wrong. What I meant was, don't touch it or all your hard work will explode, and we'll have to start over."

"It's fine," I said, taking a deep breath.

"You're the bride, Andi," Emilia said. "You don't have to apologize. There are only two times in a woman's life when she can say and do whatever the hell she wants to: on her wedding day and when she's in labor, so she should take advantage of them."

"What about when she's PMSing or going through menopause?" I asked.

Emilia considered it. "Good point. Okay, there is one day, one or two hopefully-not-too-long-or-you're-getting-the-epidural days, three to five days per month from approximately twelve to fifty-five, *and* however long it takes to go through"—she used air quotes—"the change."

"And after a bad breakup," Sara added helpfully.

"Crap! How could I have forgotten that one? Is that all of them?" Emilia waited while we all tried to think of others. "I'm going to call it. So, if you're ever bitchy when none of those exceptions are occurring, then face it—you're just a bitch."

"Thanks for clearing that up, Em. Appreciate it." A few tendrils of curls framed Andi's face in an it-looks-accidental-but-was-hard-earned twist. But what made her stunning was the nervous and excited flush on her cheeks and the honest joy in her smile.

"I'm so happy for you," I said, adjusting the shoulder strap of my bridesmaid dress. From the second I'd met Andi, I loved her. It was impossible not to. Knowing how happy she made Hayden made it even easier.

Emilia, her matron-of-honor and another woman I had instantly adored, handed me the glass of Champagne I'd put down on the vanity. Sara downed the rest of hers, grimaced, and reached for the bottle.

"Sara," Emilia snapped. "A little control would be nice. We're not here to get drunk."

"I wasn't..."

I didn't know Sara very well, partially because we hadn't spent that much time together, and partially because she seemed to be completely uninterested in letting anyone get to know her. All I knew was she had great hair, looked like a tiny human Barbie doll, worked with Andi at Emilia's virtual assistant company, and her two friends kept a close eye on her. It wasn't like they didn't trust her, more like they knew if they broke eye contact for even a second, she'd get into trouble.

"Seriously," Emilia continued, "Can you please behave for

one day? I'd like to put off the intervention until after the ceremony, at least."

"I wasn't—" Sara bit her lip, her eyes glossy and hurt-look-
ing. "I just noticed it wasn't very cold. The ice is melted... I was
going to go get more, so Andi wouldn't have to drink warm
Champagne on her wedding day." She put the bottle down on
the dresser and picked up the bucket, tilting it so we could see
the water in it. "I wasn't going to drink the whole bottle, Emilia."

Emilia glanced at Andi and sighed. "Sorry." I didn't know if
she was apologizing for what she'd said or that she was being a
little bitchy on a day she wasn't allowed to be.

"It *is* a little warm," Andi said after taking a small sip. "It'd be
great if you could get some ice, Sara. Thanks."

Trying to stay out of the drama, I sat down on the bed as
Sara passed by me silently. No smile, no *expression*, not even
anger. One foot in front of the other, eyes staring straight ahead.
It was as if as soon as she'd turned away from Emilia, all the
fight in her died. Unfortunately, if I reached out and wrapped
my arms around the poor girl like I wanted to, I was fairly sure
things would only get *more* awkward.

16

LANEY

As SOON AS the door closed behind Sara, Andi gaped at Emilia. "Holy shit, Em! What's up with you? I didn't even know you *could* be that snappy."

"Yeah, well..." Emilia sighed and looked toward the door Sara had just walked out of. "I sat next to her for the eight-hour-long plane ride. And do you know what she said to me?"

Andi and I waited, both assuming it was a rhetorical question. We were right.

"Nothing. She didn't say a single word that I didn't drag out of her. 'Yes,'" she mimicked. "'No,' and one 'great,' I think. Although, I probably misheard her. That's it." She picked up a tube of mascara, unscrewed the top, then shoved the wand back into the tube repeatedly as if she were stabbing something. "You'd be snappy too if the friend who sits in the same office you do for three days a week talks more with the UPS guy than with you."

I wondered if I should take the mascara away from her.

Before I could, Emilia leaned closer to the mirror, opened her eyes really, really wide, and brushed the wand over her top lashes. "And when she *does* talk to me, I get the only three words

I ever hear coming out her mouth nowadays. Stupid me, I'd hoped being stuck on an airplane would give us a chance to really talk about what's going on with her, but she completely shut me out."

"So you decided being a bitch to her would make her open up to you?" Andi asked.

"No," she whined, "but it should've made her react—be a bitch back to me, at least. All I want to do is help."

It wasn't my place to say anything. But today was supposed to be about Andi and Hayden, not Sara or Emilia. "She's afraid."

Both women looked at me, surprised.

"Of me?" Emilia asked.

I tilted my head side to side. "Kind of, but not. She's afraid of what you think of her. Or, more importantly, of what you'll think of her if she actually tells you what's wrong." I took a sip of my lukewarm bubbly. "I mean, I could be—and probably am—wrong, and it's definitely none of my business. But when someone you love doesn't tell you something, it's usually because they're afraid you won't love them once you know the truth." Something I'd learned from Carson, actually. One of the many things.

"Damn it," Emilia said. "So I'm basically proving her right—that I'll freak out if she tells me what's going on. Well great, now I feel awful." She raised an eyebrow, looked at Andi, then flicked her head toward me. "She's smart. Why didn't you tell me how smart she is?"

Andi smiled. "Have you met her boyfriend? Anyone who can handle that man *has* to be brilliant."

"Actually," I said, "being with Carson takes more patience than intelligence."

We all laughed at that, both of them agreeing if women really *were* smart, we would've given up on the opposite gender long ago.

When someone knocked a rhythm on the door, Emilia went to open it, pulling Sara into a bear hug as soon as she saw her. "Oh, thank goodness!"

"Uh...it's just ice, Em." Using the metal bucket as a shield between them, Sara peeked around Emilia's arm and mouthed, *Is she drunk?* to us. Andi cracked up at the expression on her face.

"Can we pretend I haven't said anything to you yet today? Whenever you're ready to tell me, I'm ready to listen. No judgment or prying. Promise."

"Okay," Sara said before mouthing, *Seriously, what's wrong with her?* "It's all good." *Should I call a doctor?*

"I mean, yes, today is one of the days I'm allowed to be a bitch—massive PMS." Emilia finally let go of her and pulled the ice bucket from Sara's clenched fingers. "But I shouldn't have taken it out on you. That's what husbands are for. Right, Andi?"

Andi swallowed and dabbed the skin under her eyes to wipe away any tears before they ruined her makeup. "I won't know for sure until five o'clock, but sure, sounds reasonable."

While Emilia and Andi joked about balls and chains, Sara and I...didn't. At least there was something we could bond over—being single. Except I wasn't actually single. I was in some kind of weird couple-limbo between being in a committed right now relationship, and a committed *forever* relationship. Both of those being completely different than *being* committed, something I imagined would happen to me eventually.

"So, Laney..." Emilia looked at me for a moment, one eyebrow raised. "Am I allowed to ask when you and Carson are tying the knot?"

Sara gasped. "Oh shit, Em! You can't ask that!"

"Why not?"

"It's like asking someone if they're pregnant!"

"It's fine." No one heard me over the chorus of arguing voices.

"That's not the same thing at all."

"Yes, it is." Sara dropped the bottle of Champagne into the bucket Emilia was still holding, grimacing as she twisted it to drive it deeper into the ice.

"No, it's not."

"How is it your business what they do?"

"How is it your business what I ask her?"

Andi pointed at me. "Guys, she's trying to talk." They didn't hear her either.

"Plus, I only asked if I was *allowed* to ask. I didn't *actually* ask."

"Seriously?" Sara yanked the bottle back out of the bucket and refilled her flute...to the brim.

"Think she knows the Champagne wasn't in there long enough to get cold?" I asked Andi loudly.

"Oh, she knows. She just doesn't care." Andi stared at her two friends with a clenched jaw.

"How would you feel if I asked you a bunch of personal things in front of other people?"

"Since we're *friends*, I'd be fine with it," Emilia snapped. "But I guess not *everyone* is like that."

"It's fine. Really," I said louder. "I don't mind."

"Would you please stop yelling at each other?" Andi yelled. I held back from laughing at the irony. "*I'm* the one who's supposed to be freaking out today, so I get to decide what I want to freak out about. And I don't choose this crap."

Both women mumbled an apology.

Andi ignored them. "Sara, if you want to fight with someone, please do it on another island."

Emilia laughed dismissively. "Maybe you should join a fight club or something—deal with those anger iss—"

"And Emilia," Andi said with just as much irritation as she'd just shown Sara, "just because we're all friends does not mean we should, or *do*, know everything about each other. Everyone is entitled to some privacy."

"Exactly!" Sara threw up her hands. "Laney, feel free to tell Emilia to shut her pie-hole. It's totally none of her—"

"Zip it!" After Andi pantomimed squeezing Sara's mouth shut, Sara shut up and downed half her Champagne in one gulp, somehow managing not to break angry eye contact with Emilia.

"I'm going to talk now, and you two are going to be quiet until further notice." She carefully placed her hands over the twist I'd worked so hard for, checking to make sure it hadn't fallen. "First of all, I agree with something Sara said. Laney, you should definitely tell Emilia to 'shut her pie-hole' but *only* because that expression is hysterical, and today is my wedding day, and I want to laugh and be happy. Second, I also agree with something Emilia said. Just asking a question doesn't make you evil."

Andi's smile broke through any past or future faux pas. "And, you know, if Laney *wanted* to answer her question…"

"Nice segue." I laughed. Andi joined me, followed by Emilia and eventually—after a quick, silent peace accord between the two women—Sara did too.

"Alright, alright," I said. It made sense they were curious. Carson and I had been together longer than Andi and Hayden had, after all. "But I don't want a big discussion about it because it's a day to celebrate you and Hayden." Not worry about Carson and me. "Overall, I've never been happier with anyone and, from what he's told me, neither has he. But we're still trying to figure out our future.

"We'll have one," I added quickly, "a great one…together. But we have some work to do before we…take the next step…" Man, was there a lot of hand movement in this explanation. A fair amount of slow, not quite understanding nods from them, too. "You know...whatever that step is...and *whenever* that step is. It'll be right...for us."

"Totally," Andi said, the others nodding and telling me what a good idea that was. Then someone suggested a toast.

I should've been a politician. I'd just said a whole bunch of absolutely nothing. But, unlike most politicians, the nothing I'd said actually made sense to someone.

"Oh no!" Sara emptied the last drop of Champagne into Andi's glass. "How many more bottles should I get?"

17

CARSON

I USED to think only women went in for all these outdated traditions. Everyone all dressed up and predictably terrified—even the people who weren't getting hitched.

I'd never admit this to anyone... ever, but I was actually into it. Historically I was the guy who made it to the bachelor party but always had a reason to skip the actual wedding.

My favorite excuse? "I'm really sorry I can't be there, but... I don't want to go."

It was as if once the sun came out, I remembered what a shitty idea marriage was and why I couldn't respect anyone who fell for the scam. So the only wedding I'd ever actually gone to —*sober*—was Hayden's first cliff dive into it. Ironically, at that one, we'd *both* known it was wrong. I'd just been the only one with enough sense to say something about it. It ended up not to be my wisest decision, though, considering how my brother was determined to go through with it and was really good at hiding how badly he didn't want to.

Since I wasn't as smart as he was, I'd ended up alone and hated by anyone who'd been within hearing distance of my big mouth. Thankfully, most of the guests had thought the honest-yet-completely-inappropriate toast I gave was a joke. Unthankfully, Hayden had known better and, after almost punching me, he'd stopped himself, deciding instead to wait until after everyone had gone to punish my face. He also gave me the silent treatment for a few months. I think that was worse than the broken nose.

But today was different. I had nothing but warm and gooey thoughts about the whole thing. Disturbingly gooey thoughts. I'd fallen for Andi just like everyone else who met her did, and I knew how happy she made Hayden. The true kind of happiness, none of that fake shit most couples slathered on and pretended was real.

I didn't even mind having to pretty myself up according to my older brother's orders. Long pants, though? On an island? What was he thinking? At least they were linen, like the shirt. Hopefully the evening breeze off the water would keep us from sweating to death.

Hayden and I were hanging out, doing nothing in his room with Emilia's husband Rob.

"Are you even allowed to have a bachelor party *after* the wedding?" I asked them. "I knew I should've just made it a surprise. That's the last time I'll ever pay attention to what *you* want. Did Andi have one?"

"You'd have to ask her." Hayden had been holding his index cards for at least an hour, sweating nervously all over them. They were probably blank anyway. Anyone who knew anything about Hayden knew he'd memorized his vows weeks ago.

"Maybe I will," I grumbled.

The women had been camped out in Andi's room since dawn, doing women things and talking about women stuff.

What *did* woman talk about for that long? Me and the other

two dicks had run through every possible topic in an hour. Now Rob and I were sitting around staring at the walls, pretending not to notice how anxious my older brother was. And forcing myself not to give him shit about it—after all, someday I might be the guy wringing my hands together and checking to make sure the ring was still there every forty-five seconds.

Shit. I'd already *been* that guy. If all went as I wanted it to, I was going to be that guy again. And again. And, if Lane ever let me knock her up, I'd be that guy at least one more time—probably more.

I needed to get out of there before I lost it.

"Well, men," I said, "I'm going to go grab us something to drink. Stretch out my legs a little," i.e., flee the awkwardness and not be there if Hayden or I had a breakdown. After promising my brother—again—that I wouldn't get either of us drunk, I headed for the bar.

Since I wasn't in a hurry to get back to the room, I leaned up against the bar and enjoyed the first swig of icy beer.

"Buy me a drink?" a woman said behind me. American accent. Shit. I would've bought everyone in the place a drink, but the last thing I needed now was to deal with a recently divorced or unhappily married woman trying to find her groove again.

Before I had a chance to come up with a nice way to tell her I didn't know where her groove was, she said, "Have you ever wondered why designers never put pockets in women's clothing?" She kept talking, not caring I'd turned around and recognized her. "My theory? It's a plot to keep us dependent on men. Or at least make us *think* we are. Same with heels. And spanks. And strapless anything."

"Sara, right?" My shoulders relaxed when she nodded. She

wasn't divorced or unhappily married, and she looked like she knew *exactly* where her groove was. Although...

Never underestimate a woman. I'd spent my formative years living down the hall from one who had an otherworldly power to locate the least available man in a room and take him down, without a single thought for the other woman involved.

"How'd you escape?" I asked.

"We ran out of Champagne. So obviously, somebody had to go in search of more. I volunteered." She was a tiny little thing, no more than five feet tall, and was wearing a very tight dress, so she had a tough time getting up onto the barstool next to me.

"Order what you need and put it on my room."

She swatted my hand down when I tried to signal to the bartender. "I'm not in a hurry. And thanks for the offer, but it's my fault we need more, so I want to pay for it myself." She paused. "Can you keep a secret?"

I nodded. "Unless it involves a felony."

"It's barely an infraction." After a quick glance around, she motioned for me to come closer. "I've been slowly emptying the bottles into the ice bucket when no one's looking. They think I'm drinking it all."

"Why would you do that?" I asked, confused.

"Because the Champagne makes the ice melt faster." She shrugged. "Empty bottle or melted ice means someone has to go in search of more."

"And being incredibly thoughtful," I said, laughing when I got it, "you always volunteer to go."

"Ta-da. I don't understand why they said you weren't smart." Before my ego had time to bruise, she giggled. "Kidding. It was something about you not being patient, I think."

"Oh, yeah, that's true."

So they were talking about me. I *knew* I was right—women *did* talk about the men who weren't around when they weren't around. Although in this case, I wasn't sure if I should be celebrating. Shit, if Lane was telling them the truth about my patience, what else was she telling them? Were they sitting around bitching about men in general? Or *me* in general? And why was I turning into someone who reacted to things they couldn't possibly know?

"I guess I'm not that smart either," I grumbled.

18

CARSON

"I DON'T DO it to feel appreciated or whatever, by the way." Sara reached across the bar and grabbed a thin cardboard coaster, then laid it over a ring of condensation my beer left. "You know, dumping the Champagne so I can volunteer to go get more. And it's not that I don't like being with them. I just need frequent breaks from all the loving relationship talk."

We both watched the water wick into cardboard.

"Huh. Too much happiness?"

"Way too much. I love them, but I knew eventually they were going to notice that I hadn't said a word about my relationship status in, like, forever and would ask me about it."

"I'm guessing your status *isn't* happy?"

"Actually, it's very happy. Because it doesn't exist. I don't begrudge them at all, but it's impossible to explain to a bunch of hens who are all madly in love that I'm glad I'm *not*."

"Well, there are a lot of cocks in the world who'd understand."

She laughed. "But you and Laney are really serious, aren't you?"

"Yeah, but we don't like to spread it around." I started wondering how much of the happy-relationship-talk Lane had been involved with again.

"That's what she said. You guys are perfect for each other."

Okay, this was slowly killing me. I wanted to ask if Lane had meant it as a joke too and what else she'd said about me. Or about marriage, weddings, proposals... anything would help at this point.

"It seems like everyone around me is either engaged or already married." Then she looked at me. "Are you guys getting engaged soon?"

"Are you phishing for intel to share with my enemies, or are you just curious?"

She smiled. "I won't share anything you don't want me to."

"Can you keep a secret?"

"Felony or misdemeanor?" Her smile faded when I took too long to answer. "Oops. I didn't mean to—"

"It's not that." I shook my head. "The truth is I want to ask her, but I don't know how." Despite Hayden's "help" earlier. "It's gotta be something great, right? Women want something memorable and romantic so they can brag to all their friends and grandkids about it. You have no idea how much pressure that puts on those of us non-romantic types."

"I'm sure you're romantic. From what I can tell, Laney is a traditionalist, right? Grew up wanting the whole fairytale romance thing? She would've given up on you a long time ago if you weren't at all romantic."

"I try to keep her so busy she doesn't notice. But I can't do that this time. It's a lot of pressure to come up with something she can brag to all of her friends about, you know?"

"Can I give you some advice?"

"Hell, yes! I was wondering when you'd pick up on all my

hints." I needed a woman's help with this, and I wasn't about to ask my stepsister. If for no other reason than Anna might deliberately suggest something horrible, and I wouldn't know any better until I'd left permanent scars on my girl.

Sara didn't know Lane all that well, but she had all the right hormones and parts. From what I could tell.

"Okay. You'll need her favorite flower—lots of them, buckets and buckets of them—your couple song if you have one..." She looked up and to the left as she switched into the language men can't understand. "Candles, maybe snacks, chocolate snacks... Oh! Glitter! Don't forget the glitter."

"Glitter?" Shit. Hayden didn't mention glitter. I *knew* I should've asked a girl first. "I should be taking notes on this, shouldn't I?"

She looked at me as if I were stupid, which, as I'd recently become aware of, was correct.

I grabbed a napkin and motioned for the bartender to come over so I could ask to borrow a pen.

"How about this? As soon as I get back to my room I'll make you a list of stuff. And then, once you have all of that and as long as what you say is true, sincere, real, and from your heart, there's no way to screw it up." She turned her head away for a second. When she turned back, her lips were pressed together tightly.

"You obviously don't know me well. I can screw anything up. It's my superpower." I was so out of my league with this.

Her brow furrowed and she pressed her lips together even tighter like she was... like she was trying to hold in—

Oh shit.

Laughter burst out of her as if it were the first time it had ever happened. "I'm sorry, but you should have seen your face!"

"Oh," I said flatly, "I can imagine."

"I'm sorry." But not sorry enough to stop laughing. "I

couldn't help it." She concentrated on not laughing, taking deep breaths and calming down... at my expense.

"Are you okay now? You sure you don't want to laugh at my pain for a little longer?"

She wiped her hand over her mouth, keeping it there until her giggles stopped. "Okay, I'm sorry. But I was trying to make a point. You don't need buckets of flowers or candles or any of that crap. I could be wrong, but she doesn't seem like the kind of girl who'd want a huge, blockbuster event. I bet what she'd really want is something special for just the two of you."

"I could've done without the laughter, but I see your point." I was thinking we were like normal couples. That definitely wasn't us.

"One more warning though: you don't want to go all the way to the other end of the spectrum. Like, for instance, when my stepdad proposed to my mom. We were at a hotel for some event I don't remember, having breakfast in our pajamas, still half asleep. He set down his cell phone for thirty seconds and said, 'Theresa, we should get married.'"

Wow. Maybe there was hope for me yet. "At least he put his phone down."

Sara grimaced. "Yeah, that was a pretty big deal for him, I guess. But don't be like Timothy—yep, grown man, worth millions, and he still goes by *Timothy*. My mom still married him, but whenever she tells anyone how it happened, she 'forgets' everything but the bizarre timing, which she thinks of as spontaneity. And then she embellishes it, like how he couldn't hold back anymore."

She pretended to swoon and then did what I assumed were highly exaggerated face and hand gestures as she pretended to be her mom. Either that, or her mom was a mime.

"He *had* to ask at that exact moment because he was over-whelmed with love." She made a gagging noise. "There's even a chance she believes it. I doubt it ever occurred to her that Timothy probably asked at that exact moment because we were already in Vegas. So he wouldn't have to take more time off work or cough up the dough for a real wedding."

"So spontaneity is good as long as it's not in Vegas. Got it." Great tip, actually. Stay away from Vegas. Make sure to put my phone down. Wait until I was overwhelmed by love—but not immediately after sex—and then segue into a proposal. It took a lot of the pressure off.

"Just be yourself," she said, "try not to use your superpower, and you'll be fine."

"If I'm not, I'm blaming you."

She snorted. "That's why I'm here." Something in the way she said it made me think I'd accidentally hit on something personal.

"So... what's your problem?"

"You can't figure it out just by looking at me?" She leaned a little backwards and held out her arms. "I'm so disappointed in you, Carson."

"Oh, man. Yeah." I grimaced. "No idea how I missed it until now. Attractive blonde wearing two-hundred-dollar shoes. Damn, you poor thing. How do you make it through the day?"

She laughed. "First of all, these shoes were only one-fifty when I bought them a few years ago, and I'd never be able to afford them now. And second, I now feel like a total shit, so thank you for reminding me of my privileged American arrogance."

"Being a privileged American myself, I felt it was my duty. After all, who else would we bother listening to?"

Her smile was shallow, not quite making it to her eyes.

"Come on, privileged girl, what's your issue?" I felt obligated to at least try repaying her for easing some of my panic.

"Well, let's see." She glanced at me and then started picking at the water-saturated edge of the cardboard coaster. "I'm all dressed up for my friend's wedding, yet instead of being there for her on her big day, I'm sitting in an empty bar with some guy I barely know, who somehow figured out how to make me feel even worse about myself."

Her wink let me know she'd meant it as a joke, at least the part about me. But it didn't cover up how much this chick could use some lessons in trust.

"What can I say? I owed you one. Speaking of..." I waved the bartender over, so she could order a drink.

We didn't speak while we watched him make the espresso she'd asked for. After he'd set the cup in front of her and wandered off again, I figured I could ask. "You said I made you feel worse. Worse than what?"

"I said that?" She dumped four silver baby-spoon-sized scoops of sugar into her coffee. "Damn. That reeks of someone hinting they want you to ask about it, doesn't it?"

This tiny woman took the world's tiniest sip of her tiny coffee, and I didn't comment. If that wasn't a sign of maturity, I wasn't capable of it.

"I'm focusing on being happy for Andi. She deserves this. I mean, there are, like, two men in the entire world as amazing as your brother."

"I'm the other, right?"

"Sure, we can go with that for now." She laughed. "I'm just going through some stuff right now, and I escaped from my friends because they all want me to talk about it. So, no offense, but even if it wouldn't bring the whole weekend down, I'm not ready to talk to anyone about it, okay?"

"Completely. Once the wedding stuff is over, will you be ready? Not to tell me, obviously, but someone?"

"I don't know." She took another tiny sip of espresso. "I told someone. It was so hard to tell her, but she... um... she didn't believe me. Or she didn't *want* to believe me. Because it would've changed everything, you know?"

"It's all a little vague to form an opinion about," I said honestly. "But I understand enough about people to know some truths are a lot harder to tell than lies. If she knows you at all..."

"I thought she did."

"Then she should've believed you. Unless you're a pathological liar or crazy."

"I'm not a liar. Crazy is subjective."

"Can't disagree there. Look, Sara, I'm the last person whose advice you should follow, but if I were you, I'd focus on finding someone you can trust. Maybe that's one of the people who are nagging you to talk about it, maybe it's not. But at least they've already proven they know you well enough to sense something's going on. Beyond the whole Champagne dumping thing, that is."

When she smiled and muttered, "You're probably right," I figured I'd done about all I could.

"One thing I've learned from years of keeping my mouth shut about the crap stuff is the only way to get past it is to let it out. It's not as if things just magically fix themselves, but keeping it all bottled up takes a shitload of energy and can really make you cranky. Think about it?"

She nodded silently.

"But don't think *too* long. The best part of life is that every day is a do-over. If we screw up today, we get another chance to make it right tomorrow."

I waved the bartender over again, pulled out some cash, and set down a healthy-sized tip onto the bar. "Put whatever else she wants on my tab."

I stopped her when she started to argue. "Back home, you

can't even make an appointment with a good therapist for less than three hundred bucks. You're *saving* me money."

I thanked her for her advice, said goodbye, and walked back to my brother's room, trying to decide if being myself was *ever* the best course of action.

As SOON AS I opened the door, Rob asked, "Where are the drinks you promised us?"

Shit, I'd been so distracted, I'd forgotten to get the only thing that was going to get me through all this. "Sorry. They fell into my mouth on the way back."

Thankfully, Hayden hadn't emptied the minibar yet, so I grabbed two handfuls of tiny bottles and sat down next to him on the couch.

"No, thanks," Hayden said, waving away liquor I hadn't intended to offer him.

"Come on. You need it." I shoved the Macallan Single Malt at him, tossed Rob a Pyrat Rum, lined up the other bottles onto the table in front of me, and cracked them all open. I did the eenie-meenie thing to see which I'd enjoy first, and boy, did I. First, a little Hennessy—always a nice way to begin the day.

I grabbed the next one—a goose of the grey variety—and took a small sip. You know, moderation and all that. "I'll be the one who gets blamed if you pass out from dehydration during the ceremony." I don't think I'd had a single sip of water since we landed. Thank the god of beer for making it mostly water, so I wasn't worried.

Hayden said a quick thanks, opened the bottle, and tipped it back, draining it in one swallow. "You're right—I did need that." Then he set the empty bottle onto the coffee table.

All three of us watched as it tipped over and fell onto the floor. Not one of us moved to get it right away. We just stared at it in silence, too preoccupied with our own issues maybe. I wasn't complaining—it was a lot better than staring at each other and feeling like we should communicate.

"What's wrong with me?" Hayden said suddenly, snapping out of the daze and picking the bottle off the floor. "I'm getting married to the woman of my dreams today. I've been looking forward to this day since the first time we spent the ni—" He cleared his throat. "Spent *time* together."

I popped a brow and looked at him. How much would I bet "spending *the ni-time* together" wasn't exactly truthful. But I appreciated his attempt to keep the conversation PG-13.

"Remember, the wedding is the hardest part, Hayden," Rob said gently. I was pretty sure Emilia said he was a lawyer, not a kindergarten teacher, but from the tone of his voice, he'd have made a great one. "Once you get past today, you'll be fine."

"I'm not nervous—I'm anxious. The *last* time I was in this position, I was nervous. Terrified, actually. But with Andi?" He shook his head. "I don't have any doubts or fears at all. Because I know, this time, it's right."

"I felt the same way with Emilia. I knew from our third date." Rob nodded his agreement, and I watched the men bond over their mutual conviction that the next forty years of their relationships would be just as good as today.

So there we were—one happily married guy, one formerly-unhappily-married/soon-to-be-happily-married guy, and... *me*. The guy who had everything he needed to be happy but who was terrified he'd blow it if he took the next step. *If* the woman he loved would take it with him.

"Did you talk to Laney last night?" Hayden asked me.

"A little. She's not a big talker *during*, you know. She tends to revert to religion—'Oh God, yes, God, yes'—and greed—'More, don't stop, give it to—'"

"Enough!" He rolled his eyes. "More than enough, actually. You promised you weren't going to talk about that to me again."

Yeah, but I didn't want to talk about Lane and me. What was there to say? We'd crashed early last night. Our first night in a tropical paradise, and I couldn't touch her. That fucking jellyfish had ruined everything. But I couldn't complain about not getting laid enough. Especially not to a man about to go through a ceremony that, from the horror stories I'd heard, was the first stop on the never-having-sex-again train.

"I don't remember promising anything," I said. "Besides, why do you want to talk about me and Lane now? We should be talking about happy things."

Rob turned toward me. "You two are having problems?"

Great. Now both of them were focused on me. "We're fine. Really. Maybe a little off in our wavelengths, but it won't last. We're here, on a beautiful island, in a beautiful country, for the wedding of my beautiful brother and his fiancée." The back of my hand slammed into Hayden's chest as I gesticulated wildly to get my point across. "We're going to enjoy the beautiful stuff and figure out the crappy stuff after we get home."

Rob nodded. At least one of us understood. "Just don't wait too long, Carson. No matter how committed two people are, it's impossible to be together for a long amount of time without any conflict. The trick is to deal with the issues while they're still small. If you wait, shit builds up, and it takes a whole lot of work to fix it. That's when an unbiased third-party should step in."

"I thought you were a lawyer, Rob, not a shrink."

"Sometimes it's the same thing," he mumbled. Maybe he was hoping this would turn into a working vacation, and he'd get to write it off on his taxes. "I didn't mean to pry. And enjoying today is equally important."

"Ignore my brother, Rob. Carson isn't used to people actually wanting him to be happy."

I stopped myself from responding snidely when I realized the truth of it. Everyone who gave a shit about me was currently on this small pocket of land in the Southern Pacific Ocean. And the only person who'd never given up on me—not once—was a few doors down with the estrogenic half of this party.

Lane had *never* stopped wanting me to be happy, even when she thought that meant *she* had to be *unhappy*.

"You're right." I stood up so quickly, my knee slammed into the table, knocking all the bottles over. The other men jumped out of their seats and away from the liquid, probably afraid they'd smell like booze and have to wear board shorts to the ceremony instead of our fancy pants.

Hayden cursed at me and Rob ran for a towel, while I stood still and let my mind figure it out by itself. I've always found it better to just let it do its thing rather than force it to do the *smart* thing.

"You're right. She wants me to be happy. And there's only one way I will be."

"I hope that made sense to you because I have no idea what you're talking about."

That was okay. He didn't need to understand. Only *she* did.

I apologized as I ran. "I'll be right back. Swear."

The main section of the resort was small, but all the damn doors looked exactly the same. Some of them must've been storage, the laundry room, or just haunted.

But Lane was behind one of them, sitting there, not knowing what I had suddenly realized. I had to find her.

Be myself. Women loved spontaneity. I didn't bring my phone, so that was good. Be myself. I was so overwhelmed by love, I would've kicked down all those doors to find her if I had to.

Or I could, you know, say her name.

"Lane," I called at a normal volume. When none of the doors opened, I called again, louder this time. "Lane! Lane, where are you? I need to ask you something!"

As soon as I heard movement to my right, I spun toward it and practically knocked the guy over as the door opened.

I stopped as soon as I saw him. "You're not my girlfriend."

"Thankfully, no," the man said as he righted himself and slammed the door back in my face.

"Lane!"

Another door, farther down the hallway opened, and I heard her say, "Carson? Is everything okay?"

I ran over and bounded into the room as she backed away from me. The other women were all standing, looking alarmed, and I had a moment of regret. There probably was a better way to handle this. With a few less eyes on me. But I was flying high on my realization, feeling invincible, like no one could possibly refuse me, especially Lane.

"What's wrong?" Andi rushed forward, holding her skirt in her fists. "Is Hayden—?"

"Fine. Hay's fine. Super excited to get going. Are you guys ready yet?" I smiled. Fairly pathetically.

"Carson, you shouldn't be here right now," Lane said, pushing my arm.

"Why not? *We're* not getting married." The whole think-before-you-speak thing was new to me, and something I hadn't yet mastered. Evident in the communal gasp and pitying glances at Lane. It still took a few more seconds until I'd processed all the worst things only women could've read into my comment.

"I didn't mean we're *never* getting married." I looked around the room, hoping to see a supportive face. Someone to tell me to stop talking before I *really* said something I'd regret. "I just meant I can see the bride. 'Cause you're not the bride...yet. I don't mean—"

"Go away, Carson." Lane shut her eyes for a second and then shoved me backwards. "This isn't the right time." Then she whispered. "Today isn't about our shit. Go tell your brother we'll be ready in about forty-five minutes."

"I will but, before I go, I really need to ask you something."

Over Lane's shoulder, I saw Sara. Her eyes were huge, like a cartoon character whose foot just got squished by an anvil. She shook her head and mouthed something. All I got was "...superpower."

Oh shit. I was using my superpower—if there was a way to screw something up, I'd be the one to find it. I should've known being myself wouldn't work.

I shut my mouth and let Lane push me out the door, mumbling a quick apology and internally slapping myself for almost ruining yet another moment that should've been special. Just not for me.

20

CARSON

AFTER I LEFT THE WOMEN, I'd gone back to the guys' room, drank all the liquor that hadn't spilled from the little bottles, and lamely told my brother everything was okay and my flip out had nothing to do with him or Andi.

An hour of uncomfortable discussion about how great marriage was later, I stood next to my brother, who was fidgeting impatiently, waiting for this thing to get started.

Lane was right—today wasn't about me. Occasionally being able to forget that was one of my less admirable talents. I'd been alone so long, I needed a kick in the head. A strong reminder the world didn't revolve around me, and other people's needs were, in fact, more important sometimes.

So I vowed not to misbehave anymore and to focus on being the *best* best man I could for my brother.

"Please tell me you didn't forget the ring," Hayden whispered out of the side of his mouth.

I tapped my pocket until I felt the curve of metal, assuring both of us I hadn't fucked up something else. "Got you covered, bro."

Andi had wanted a small wedding, and that's what this was.

She'd been raised by her grandmother who'd passed away, and the only family she had were her closest friends. So the small group of gawkers didn't exactly follow the seating rule about making guests decide if they liked the bride or the groom more.

Sara, Rob, and Hillary sat on Andi's side. Since I'd spent most of my life wishing I had no family, I pretended not to see Renee and Anna in the seats right in front of where Hay and I stood. Every once in a while, I heard Renee sniffle, as if she were already overcome with emotion. As if she *had* emotions. My guess—she was overwhelmed with shock that two people were getting married for the *right* reasons.

Eric was walking around with a camera stuck to his face, capturing who knew what—how bored we all were waiting for Andi to come out maybe?

Clare was rushing up and down the aisle, kicking up sand and holding a tablet that, to my knowledge, was only for show. There were only five people in the wedding party—my brother, Andi, Emilia, Lane, and me. And I was pretty sure we all already knew what we were supposed to do.

Stand there. Smile. Keep the groom from fainting, and make sure the best man doesn't make any inappropriate comments. Clare would've been better off bringing a roll of duct tape.

At about twenty minutes before sunset on this tropical island, the only one who wasn't sweating was the man who would be performing the ceremony standing beneath an arch of flowers. Not only had he been through more marriages than all of us combined—even when my mother was included in the scenario—the officiant was local and used to the heat.

Finally, Clare nodded to the solo violinist Hayden had flown in from somewhere off island. Since the musician was male, under seventy-five, and only here for today, he couldn't have been any more perfect for my stepsister. When she saw him, I thought I actually heard Anna's completely-unsuitable-for-a-relationship alarm go off. When the guy went home, he'd have a wallet full of cash, a smile on his face, and a hell of a story to tell.

Truthfully, the man was worth every penny and sexual favor he might get. I've never been a classical music kind of guy, but I knew when something was done right. Somehow, each note carried over the rhythmic sound of the waves and the ripple of wind through the palm trees, as if the entire island had decided to accompany him.

I heard another sniffle, but didn't look. Mostly because, at that moment, the most beautiful woman I'd ever seen came out from behind the wicker panel at the far end of the aisle. Hot damn. Lane's smile was like sunlight, her dark eyes shining like the ocean at night.

Yep, at that moment, I understood. I could finally make sense of all those poets I used to make fun of.

Lane ducked her head shyly, lifting the side of her dress and flicking it out until it caught the breeze. She reached into the little basket she was carrying and grabbed a handful of pink petals, tossing them onto the sand as she walked.

Emilia came out next, wearing a similar dress but nowhere near as well. Not that she wasn't a beautiful woman, but...

Nah, nobody had ever looked as good as Lane did. When my girl reached the archway and sat in the seat next to Hillary, I grumbled, unable to see her through my brother's head.

Emilia took her spot across from me just as the violinist paused. Poking her head out of the bamboo screen, Clare made eye contact with the musician. She nodded to him and ducked back behind the screen as he began playing the old-school wedding song. Then another beat came on, coming from speakers set up just behind the violinist. The new, synthesized music worked with the notes of the violin, not overpowering them.

I knew I wasn't imagining it when the people sitting down

started looking around to find out where the music was coming from. It fit the couple perfectly.

Hayden was a traditionalist, always had been. Andi brought a bit of unpredictability to his life, along with more fun and excitement than I'd thought he could handle. They'd never tried to change each other, all the positive strides they'd made had happened just by having someone who loved them at every step along the way.

Andi stepped out and stood at the end of the aisle while Clare fluffed out the back of her dress. There was no big tail-thing on it that would drag on the ground behind her, but it seemed like dress fluffing was a tradition.

When Clare whispered "Okay," Andi started walking. By herself. Without a father or uncle to give her away, she'd chosen to walk alone. And it made perfect sense. She was coming into this screwball family of her own volition, and Hayden wasn't the only Bennett who loved her.

When I looked toward where Lane was seated, I noticed my brother—the reason I was there. His eyes were cartoonishly large, his hands fisted at his sides.

"Hayden," I whispered. "Breathe." Then I remembered something I'd promised Andi to make sure wouldn't happen. "Don't lock your knees, bro. I'm not sure I'm up to catching you." Damn, I thought she'd been joking.

"Breathe," he mouthed, pulling in air through his teeth. "Right."

"Nice breathing, man. Keep it up." I patted him on his shoulder and then kept my hand up, an inch or so from his back, just in case. "Remember to keep your knees unlocked. You're doing great."

"Great." He drew the word out as he slowly exhaled. When he smiled, I wondered if he'd maybe gotten *too* much oxygen. "Have you ever seen anything more beautiful, Carson?"

I let out a sigh of relief. "She's gorgeous, Hay." Almost as beautiful a bride as my Lane would be someday. "You're a lucky guy."

He nodded slowly and, if I looked at him for more than a second, I might've sworn I saw water in his eyes. But the breeze was picking up, so some sand had probably blown into his eyes.

"I never thought I'd be here, Carson. Not feeling like this. I never thought I *could* feel like this."

"As long as you don't feel like you're going to faint, it's all good, bro."

After Andi handed her bouquet to Emilia and her dress had been fluffed out again, she took the last few steps that brought her to Hayden.

"Hello, Mr. Bennett," she whispered, smiling. "You're not going to pass out, are you?"

He laughed quietly as he took her hands. "Nothing in the world would keep me from making you mine. Not today. Not tomorrow. Not ever."

Good answer. But I glanced down at his legs anyway—his knees might've had other ideas, and it was my job to keep him standing.

21

CARSON

I ADMIT to missing the beginning bits where the officiant said a bunch of crap about love, family, and commitment. I had an important job to do, and my brother was counting on me. So since it was a short ceremony, I missed most of it.

"...and I could be that woman, because you believed in her. Because you believed in *me*," Andi said, smiling nervously. She glanced at the officiant, who nodded. "*Sooo*, I promise to always love, respect, and *occasionally* obey you. But only when I feel like it and you say 'please.'"

She waited until everybody was done laughing. "Your turn."

Hayden took a deep breath. "Anyone who knows me at all knows I worked on my vows for the last six weeks and memorized every word until I could recite them in my sleep. But at this very moment, in front of you and the people we care about, I seem to have forgotten what I'd planned to say."

Oh shit. Was it in my job description to whisper his lines in his ear if he forgot them? Clear as day, I could see those index cards, resting in one neat pile on the coffee table back in the room. I worked out the math—speed x distance x panic. It would take me about three minutes to sprint there, grab the cards, and run back.

But Hayden wasn't done talking. "And I don't think there's a more apropos way to start my life with you than having to wing it."

Andi ducked her head and laughed quietly.

"Andi?" Hayden reached out and gently lifted her chin. "I've spent my whole life priding myself on being able to handle anything that came at me, logically, rationally, without fear. But then you appeared, and I wasn't prepared for it. There was nothing logical, or even rational, in how I felt about you. And it terrified me. But something in me, the intuition I'd never really trusted, wouldn't stop screaming, 'She's worth it.'"

Andi's lip trembled as he spoke honestly, without pride or arrogance. With more vulnerability than I thought my brother capable of. As if they were the only two people talking. As if they were the only two people on this island.

"You knocked me out of a life I was barely living, Andi, and showed me what was possible. Convinced me that not always being in control, or knowing what would happen, was a gift. Every day since then has been more than I ever imagined it could be, and I'll spend the rest of my life making sure you feel the same way." My brother sounded so calm, so sure, I knew if I looked at anyone else, they'd be crying.

I only heard bits and pieces of the rest of the vows Hayden and Andi had written for each other. I should've at least been paying attention so I didn't miss my cue, but all I could focus on was my girl.

Lane hadn't looked at me once, entirely focused on the couple we were here to celebrate. But when Hayden cleared his throat, she blinked away some tears, and I finally caught her eye. We stared at each other, a sense of peace falling over me as I realized this was it. This was *everything*.

I swear, I felt so much damn gooeyness, if I took a step, I'd leave a snail trail of goodwill behind me.

Shit, I even loved my *family* right then. Granted, it would only last until I actually *spoke* to one of them again, but still...

Life could never be better than this.

With my eyes still locked onto her, I started imagining this was our wedding day and the officiant was talking directly to us. Any second he'd say, "Do you, Carson, take this woman—?"

"Hell, yes." *Fuuuuuuck*. That was out loud.

Everyone looked at me confused, annoyed, or both. I tried to remember what they'd been saying, what I'd agreed to. Oh shit, what if it was the if-anyone-has-a-problem-with-these-two-people-getting-hitched part?

Hayden was standing there, holding out his hand. "Great. Then how 'bout you give it to me?"

Lane looked exasperated. She was frantically mouthing something to me in a language that couldn't possibly be English, because I had no idea what she was trying to tell me. Then she drew a circle in the air.

"What does that mean?"

"The ring, Carson," Hayden said quietly. "You need to give me the ring now."

"Oh! Yeah. Hell, yeah." Relieved, I fumbled to find it, checking my pants first, then remembering I'd put it into the inside pocket of my jacket. "Got it!" I held it up in the air proudly like a kid who'd lost their first tooth.

Good thing Hayden's default reaction to calamity was calm. Good thing that was his default reaction to everything I did. Although today, he was rightfully nervous too, which affected his patience with his little brother.

"*Now*, Carson."

I carefully set the ring in his hand, knowing the only thing that could make this moment worse was if I dropped it, then accidentally stepped on it while trying to pick it up, and had to shovel into the sand to find it again. Of course, those kinds of things only happened to people in movies... and to me. And usually it would crack me up, but times had changed. I wasn't the only person I cared about anymore.

They did the whole "with this ring" bit, and it was time for them to kiss. My consistently controlled and subdued brother turned into someone with a wild side. He didn't grab her and shove his tongue in her mouth or anything. Nah, this kiss was slow, sensual, full of a lot more passion than I was comfortable seeing, at least when the guy was my brother.

It was the kind of kiss women turned away from to give the couple a little privacy and men watched out of their peripheral vision.

I stared at my feet until I heard everybody clapping and a few catcalls.

Hallelujah! I made it—*we* made it—through the whole cere-mony without any fainting or disaster. And all the tears shed were from happiness and sentimentality, even from Renee.

Friends and family attacked the couple before they'd gotten a few steps down the aisle, turning Andi and Hayden in every direction for a kiss on the cheek or a hug or a handshake.

Lane walked around the group to stand next to me and slip her arm around my waist.

"Did I see you cry?" she whispered to me.

I didn't think so, but I checked my lower eyes lashes anyway. Anything could've happened while I was in fantasy land. "Maybe—men always cry when we lose another good one."

Luckily, my lashes were dry. But hers weren't.

"Same thing with women, huh?" When I slowly brought my thumb to her eye, she closed them for me so I could wipe away the tears that hadn't already dried on her cheeks.

"Something like that." She gave me a quick kiss then waded

into the crowd to congratulate the bride and groom. I decided I'd do it later, once I figured out why they deserved congratulations to begin with. Saying some nice things and signing a piece of paper wasn't exactly as impressive as running a marathon or winning the Nobel Peace Prize. Although, maybe that was the point—marriage was like running a marathon for forty, fifty years and you'd never make it that long unless you'd figured out how to keep the peace.

22

CARSON

WITH SUCH A SMALL GROUP, the reception felt more like spending the day somewhere beautiful with good friends, along with a few people I'd be happy to live without, than any wedding I'd ever been to, crashed, or dodged.

"What's happening?" I asked Rob when Andi told all the single ladies to stand about ten feet away from her. A very selective group—only Lane, Sara, Anna, Hillary, and Clare—stood together and sang the only two lines they knew from the Beyoncé song.

"Andi's going to throw the bouquet."

"Where?"

He looked at me with equal confusion. "Haven't you ever been to a wedding before?"

"Sure, but I'm usually drunk by this point." Or, long ago, hooking up with a bridesmaid, something that would be happening again as soon as I could get Lane alone.

Rob's expression didn't change.

I shrugged. "If you knew my mother, you'd understand." I'd been to three of her weddings. Being sloshed was the only way I got through them without saying anything honest about Renee and her taste in husbands.

"The bride tosses the bouquet and, supposedly, whoever catches it will be the next to get married."

"And that makes sense to people? Still?"

"Not really, but it's tradition."

Right. But just in case there was any truth to it, I let out a sigh of relief Renee hadn't joined the others. My mother was a recovering addict. It had been over two years since she'd worn an engagement or wedding ring, but it was better if she stayed away from temptation entirely.

I looked at Andi as she turned her back on the women. Aside from Hillary, none of them looked too happy to be there. Earlier in the bar, I'd learned just enough about Sara to guess she wasn't dating anyone. But in case of doubt, the way she had to be shoved into the group and had her hands glued to her sides were good indicators. Clare was busy organizing the others, herding them closer together and making sure Eric had a clear view for photos.

The most shocking thing was to see Anna mildly into it. My guess? She didn't give a shit about the tradition. She saw it as competition and therefore, it was something she had to win. And Lane? Well, Lane was subdued, even as Clare pushed her up front.

After one more quick glance behind her, Andi counted down, swinging her arm as if she were warming up for a toss from the outfield. "Three...two...one!"

Then, still clutching her bouquet, she turned around and ran over to the group, shoving the flowers right at Lane. Everyone laughed, including me, until I remembered what that actually meant.

Lane's cheeks turned red as everyone applauded, and I felt someone smack me on the back.

"Pressure's on now, little brother," Hayden whispered in my ear.

Now? Did he mean I should do it right now, in front of everybody? Why else would he have used the word? I didn't have to worry about flowers because Lane was already holding some.

I took it as another sign when my knee buckled underneath me. I could do this. And if she said no, I would still have enough adrenaline and leftover positive feelings to swim back to California.

"What the hell are you doing?" Hayden dragged me up.

"What do you mean? You said *now*!"

"Oh, Carson. You need help."

Yeah, that's what I thought I was getting. From him. Then I saw Lane again, the tiny shakes of her head as she tried to push the flowers into somebody else's hands, the whispered "No," and the way she kept trying to redirect focus back onto Andi.

I tried not to think too hard about what it all meant.

As the servers came out with trays of food, everybody dispersed to sit down around wood tables set-up on a shaded patio ten feet away from the sand and help themselves to the Champagne. I looked around for Lane and saw her a little farther down the beach, facing the ocean and picking at one of the flowers in the bouquet.

"Will he or will he not?" I said quietly, coming up behind her and slipping my arms around her.

"It doesn't mean anything, Carson. Don't worry."

I turned her around, then lifted her chin until she was looking into my eyes. "I'm not worried. Never have been."

"Well, you should be," she said, her smile finally showing up.

"Aww, it's our first threat. Someone take a picture!" I looked around for the photographer.

Clare was leading Eric around as she positioned people into various fake-candid poses.

"Hey, you!" I yelled at her. "Lady with the control issues! We need someone to take a selfie for us!"

Lane laughed under her breath, knowing exactly how I felt about men and that whole obsession. Instead of "selfies," I called them "total dick pics." Because only a *total dick* would think anyone wanted to see him flexing in front of a mirror or sitting in his car.

Clare turned away from the tableau involving Andi and Renee, quickly ordered them to look happy, and started walking toward us. Eric had better turn his shutter speed all the way up, because Hayden's new bride felt the same way about her new mother-in-law as everyone else in the family did. Plus, Renee's sincerity could only last about as long as a teenage boy the first time he got laid.

Clare smoothed her hair back as she neared us. "Who knew weddings were so stressful?"

"Um... you?" Lane's voice rose at the end of the word, turning it into a question.

"True. But in my defense, I was stressed out for far less pleasant reasons at *my* wedding."

"Because you'd just realized you were going to have to put up with my brother forever?"

She winked. "Something like that."

"Can we get a picture of Lane and me on the beach? We're celebrating a moment."

Her eyes got huge.

"Yep," I said, waiting for her disappointment to set in. "Lane just threatened me. I figure someday the picture can either make us laugh or be used as evidence in her trial."

Lane studied me. "You say that as if you think I'm not smart enough to make it look like an accident."

"Oh, you're smart enough. But there's no such thing as a perfect crime, and I don't want you going to prison for doing the right thing."

Clare shook her head. "You guys are so perfect for each other. Come on, let's find a better background for the picture."

"And something that could be used as a weapon." Lane laughed as we followed Clare around and heard her complain about the sunset. Apparently it had purposefully shown up on the wrong side of the island, just to ruin all the shots she'd planned.

She called Eric on her walkie talkie—yes, I'm serious—to let him know he was needed and where. Twenty seconds later, he was jogging toward us, anxious to prove his worth to my ex-sister-in-law. The little business she'd started with Hayden's help had already grown large enough to need employees and a solid list of freelancers.

Lane and I let Clare position and reposition our bodies, step back to contemplate our humiliation, then shake her head sadly as she came in for another round. She twisted my shoulders, moved my hand off Lane's ass—

"Ah, come on! That's its comfort zone!"

—and told us to smile without showing any teeth.

"Stop sneering, Carson. Tilt your head a little to the left, Laney. And lift your chin." Obviously we were idiots because she actually showed us how to do every motion as she listed it. "Maybe... um..."

Lane held onto my arm for life when Clare knocked the back of her knee so her hip stuck out and she stopped standing "like a sumo wrestler."

"Clare, if you really want to show off Lane's *best* side, you need to turn her away from the camera."

The women didn't find my comment nearly as funny as Eric did. I think Lane would've if she hadn't been worried laughter would ruin Clare's hard work and force us to start over.

"Great. Now look natural."

Lane and I glanced at each other from the corner of our eyes.

"Is this how it's gonna be at your wedding?" I asked her through my teeth.

Lane was a better ventriloquist than me. "You mean if I ever find someone worth marrying?"

I tried not to smile. "I was trying to be supportive, but yeah, if you can ever find someone who'll love your sorry ass."

"It's not my ass I'm worried about."

"Carson, stop fidgeting please," Clare said, in between comments to Eric about good angles. "We're almost done. Just want to get a few more."

This was a huge mistake. I'd just wanted a picture I could use as a screensaver, not to submit to *National Geographic*. Plus, I was now one hundred percent sure I could hear the bar calling my name.

"To answer your question," Lane whispered. "I think I'd prefer something a little more casual."

"Vegas is casual," I joked, knowing how much she hated the place.

"Sure, if I meet him at a Vegas strip club or something, then that might work. As long as it's somewhere that means something to us. And is family-friendly."

"That takes me out of the running—there isn't a place on earth where my family is friendly."

"Stop it. My cheeks are cramping."

"You sure? I should check." I slipped my hand from her waist down to its comfort zone and gave her cheek a little squeeze. "Feels good to me."

Her ass tightened beneath my hand. "Owww!" she wailed.

Shit, the jellyfish sting! "Sorry, babe. Look but don't touch."

How could I have forgotten the world's most depressing expression?

"Carson!" Clare yelled. "That was *almost* the perfect shot."

I shook out my arms and watched Lane try to twist around to look at the source of her pain.

"Why do I get blamed whenever someone does something inappropriate?"

"Because you're always the *someone*," Lane said, still gently rubbing her ass.

"I cannot be held responsible for the temptation created by your proximity."

I held her face in my hand and leaned down to kiss her. The parting of her lips was all the invitation I needed to deepen the kiss and forget where we were.

Somewhere in the distance, I heard Clare gasp and say, "Perfect! Stay just like that."

Gladly. In fact, I planned to stay just like this as often as I could for the rest of my life.

23

LANEY

OUR ORIGINAL PLAN had been to stay on the island a few more days and have some fun. Unfortunately, any fun we might have had was curtailed by the fact that I still couldn't sit down without wincing. So any excursion we could've gone on was out of the question, and I was too afraid to go back into the water. Carson and I tried all kinds of convoluted sexual positions, but —shocker—even if your butt isn't *directly* involved in the position, it's still involved.

I finally decided I just wanted to go home, get one of those awful butt pillows, and recover a little dignity before the unveiling of my lobby piece. So I asked the concierge to move up our flight home. We could leave on the same flight most of the other wedding guests would be on. Carson wasn't thrilled to be on the same flight as Renee and Anna, or Hillary and Eric for that matter, but he agreed as soon as I started crying.

I looked at my boarding pass again, then turned it over as if it would say something different on the back.

Damn it. "These are the wrong tickets. The guy said the other flight had room on it. So how'd we get the wrong ones?" We were on a different flight than everyone else and had a layover. If the flight had sold out, why didn't the concierge tell me?

I put my anger on pause when I saw Carson's face. He had on his I'm-lying-but-feel-bad-about-it expression.

"Carson?" I spoke slowly, not wanting to spook him. "Did you have our tickets changed?"

He stared at me silently for a minute, then wet his lips. "Possibly. But if I did, I would have had a really good reason to."

"Right." I only needed one guess as to why. "Carson, did you put us on a longer flight just to avoid being on the same one as Hillary and Eric? Or was it Renee and Anna you wanted to avoid?"

He put his hand on his heart, a hurt expression on his face. "Babe, do you really think I would do—?" He cursed when he broke, his smile huge. "I would definitely do something like that, wouldn't I? But I didn't this time. Swear it."

He held his left hand over my ticket and raised up his right as if taking an oath on a bible. "I didn't change the tickets just to avoid being on the same flight as all the people I dislike hanging out with most. Promise. That said, I can't guarantee I won't find anyone to dislike during the flight. Especially if they steal the armrest."

"Then why did you change the reservation?"

"Surprise?" he said weakly.

"What kind of surprise?"

"We have a layover now."

"Oh! You meant a *shitty* surprise."

"That's not—" He shook his head. "We have a layover... in San Diego."

I grew up in San Diego. My parents still lived there. So the surprise was... "Why?"

"Well, because I talked your mom down from a two-week

visit to a three-day visit. Without insulting her or even *mentioning* sex toys."

"You spoke to my mom?"

He nodded. "And I asked her to get you a butt pillow. Didn't tell her why, though. Shit, will she think I was asking for a sex toy when I said 'butt pillow'?"

"No, she'd think a butt pillow was for hemorrhoids. So you implied I have hemorrhoids. To my mom."

"Uh... maybe?" He ran his hand through his hair nervously. "Did I make a huge mistake?"

"About the pillow?" I stammered. "I wouldn't call it a *huge* mistake, but... I'm just..." Deep breath. "Are you sure you want to meet them?"

"Yes and no. But a lot more yes than no." He grimaced. "That's not exactly right either. If you want, I could lay out my pros and cons list for you. I can recite it from memory."

I kissed him, knowing what it symbolized for him. Knowing that he was putting aside his issues with his own parents and wanted to meet mine because it was the next step for us. How could I complain about that?

The only problem was I also knew what it meant for *me*. And that was a lot more complicated and a lot less sweet.

At least we could fight about which one of us was more nervous. Don't get me wrong—my parents are good people. They're just not *Carson* people. I still didn't understand why they ever moved from the East Coast to California, let alone had lived there happily for thirty years. Neither of them understood sarcasm. *Both* of them assumed everyone who wore ripped jeans and had a band's name on their t-shirt needed a hot meal and a place to sleep.

I was fifteen before I realized what that confused look on strangers' faces meant. The one that appeared right after my mom gave them some money or one of the homeless care packages we made up every Sunday after church. I'm sure they enjoyed the sandwich, but ninety-nine-point-nine percent of them *weren't* homeless. They were just fashionably dressed young people hanging out in downtown San Diego. I couldn't count how many times I'd explained they didn't need combs—they wore their hair like that on purpose. My parents would smile and hug me, but they never believed me.

"My parents are really nice people."

"I'm sure they are." Carson gave me the confused look I'd seen so often in my teens but eventually, his smile took over. "I mean, after screwing up their daughter so badly and siccing her on the rest of the world, they have a lot to make up for."

I slugged him in the gut. Unfortunately his laughter had tightened his abs and protected him from any real damage.

"Do you really want to start down the road of whose parents have more to make up for?" It was meant to be a joke, but nothing about his parents made him laugh, unless bitter laughs counted.

He shrugged it off. "Since you don't have a sibling to counter your horribleness, I think I'm still ahead. Plus, any damage I reap upon the world is taken care of by lawyers and non-disclosure agreements." He pointed to himself with both thumbs. "Winner and still champion."

"Is there anything you *don't* win?"

"You mean that I *want*? Let's see. Nope. I even won you. That's a biggie."

"Thanks," I muttered. "As if I'm such a great prize."

"The biggest. Someday, you'll make all the other trophy wives hide their Ferragamo purses and Gucci heels in shame."

I gasped. "I'm not a trophy wife!"

"Not yet." The bastard smirked.

"I swear to you right now, in front of all these people we'll probably never see again, I will never be a silent smile-and-nod fixture on your arm, Carson Bennett."

"What about in my bed? I never want you to be silent, but I kind of love the smile and nod thing you do when you come. Usually your eyes are rolled back in your head and it's not so much a *smile* as it is a—Oof! That hurt!" Because he hadn't tightened his abs yet. He rubbed where my hit had landed.

"Serves you right."

"Come on, babe! You know I'm kidding. I would never want you to be anything other than who you are—a strong, opinionated woman who looks amazing when she comes and can throw a decent punch."

"Better remember that."

His comeback—which I'm sure would've been something I'd have to pretend offended me and didn't make me want to laugh —was cut off by the overhead announcement.

"Flight 1025 to San Diego, California is now boarding at Gate 2. Now boarding first-class passengers and those who need extra time. Please have your boarding passes and passports out."

"Hurry, before they run out of ass pillows." As Carson gathered our bags and mumbled something snide about my impressive ability to over pack, I wondered if I'd ever get tired of his unpredictability. Doubted it. Seriously, seriously doubted it.

24

CARSON

I'D BEEN in worse situations. Couldn't think of any at the moment... or for the last few months, but hey, I'm sure there had been some.

It wasn't as if I didn't know how to behave properly around people. But the families the Bennett Foundation helped were easier. First off, the only reason we ever met was because they had a really sick kid. Chronic childhood illness could knock an inappropriate joke out of anybody with half a soul, including me.

Secondly, because of the programs we offered and the help we gave, those parents would've pretended to like me even if I were a car dealer.

Thirdly, and possibly most importantly, they seemed to actually like my sense of humor—the one tempered for the under-eighteen crowd, obviously. Plus, kids were just easier to be around than adults, I guess. Especially since the only adults I'd ever wanted to impress just happened to be anxiously waiting for any of my many faults to slip out.

Lane's grip wasn't helping either. She'd taken hold of my hand as soon as the plane landed and hadn't let go since. Not easy to grab our bags off the carousel one-handed, by the way. Or with a slippery palm. Or with a girlfriend who was evidently as nervous as I was.

I shook my hand out of hers to shift one bag so I could set the other one onto the cart.

"So, are you nervous *for* me or *because* of me?" I asked.

She didn't have time to answer, I guess. All that frantic glancing around in a minor panic could eat up your whole day.

"Babe? *I'm* the one who's supposed to be scared. Not you. And your freak-out is starting to make me think there's something you're not telling me."

She went from sixty to zero in five and slowly turned toward me. "Okay, don't be mad..."

Ugh.

"You know how I told you my parents are conservative?" She paused just to make the impact more painful, maybe. "I didn't actually tell them we were living together."

Oh. That wasn't too bad. Definitely not the first time a girl had lied to her parents about me. Granted, I was a little surprised *Lane* had done it. She wasn't the kind of woman who lied—even by omission—but I'd had to sit through enough bad movies about women and their overprotective, doting, clueless, and often violent, gun-toting fathers to know—

Fucking hell. This was a bad idea. I shouldn't leave the airport. No guns allowed, metal detectors and security guards everywhere.

Plus, if the perp brought you to the second location... *Never* let them take you to the second location!

"And—" she started.

Oh shit, there was more!

"—I probably should've mentioned this before, but..."

"But what, Lane? But *what*?"

"Laney!" someone called.

Lane flinched and swung toward the attractive fifty-something couple coming toward us. The woman waved with the ass pillow she held up. Didn't see that every day. But I recognized them from Lane's pictures. Sure, her dad had a little more belly and a lot more forehead than he'd had when the picture Lane kept in our living room was taken. And her mom's hair was shorter and darker. But overall, they looked just as normal in person—nice, average people.

The only issue was the really bad feeling I had over whatever Lane had left out of all the previous conversations we'd had about her parents.

"What should you probably have mentioned earlier, Lane?" I asked quickly.

She glanced at me, her smile pasted on and nervous.

"Put me out of my misery here, woman."

"Well," she said, still waving to her parents, who'd just gotten caught by the crowd. "My father might still be under the impression I'm a virgin, and the man I'm with respects my decision."

I swallowed my laugh. She wasn't kidding. "Oh, I respect your decisions, babe. Completely. For instance, I respected your decision to ride me like a cowgirl the other night. And I had all kinds of respect for you when you dragged me into that restaurant bathroom a couple weeks ago because you needed to fuck right then and there. And the thing you did with your tongue the other—"

She shushed me with an elbow to the ribs. So more like a shut-the-fuck-up tap.

"How much did you actually tell them about me?"

"Lots of good things."

It was always her pauses that worried me. And the longer they were, the more concerning.

"I just may have forgotten to mention anything... they could use to look you up. And I also might have accidentally mispronounced your last name so they couldn't guess how it was spelled."

As insulting as that was, it was also smart. Typing my name into a Google search was something I'd never had the courage to do. If half the shit I'd done was on there, it would only scar her folks and make them hate me. Better to let them figure out they hated me in *person*. Wait a second...

Nope, no time for waiting. It was time to meet the parents.

After the first round of family hugs, Lane said, "Mom? Dad? This is Carson."

"Good to finally meet you, son," her dad said. I hadn't felt such a firm handshake since... never. But it was the fact he'd called me *son* that rendered me speechless. Unless you counted the grunt I let out when Lane's mom pulled me into a bear hug, the ass pillow smooshed between us.

"I'm so glad you're here," she said, not letting go. I carefully put my arms on her mid-back, not wanting to accidentally brush anywhere I shouldn't on the way around. "Thank you so much for coming."

I'd heard of people like this but had never met any of them. *Real* people. People who'd never understand why anyone would feel more comfortable kissing the air near someone's cheek than getting some skin in the game and actually *touching*. People who accepted someone just because their daughter had left out all vital, truthful, and identifiable information about him.

I'm not sure why Lane was so worried. They were great. I just had to be myself. Mostly. I just had to be the *good* part of myself. The well-behaved part. It might be shriveled and rusty from non-use, but I could do it.

After all, it was only a few days, right? I could be not-me for a few days.

Lane glanced back at me with an apologetic look as her mom ushered her out of the baggage area, leaving her dad

—"Call me Bill"—and I to bring the bags. Our talk was kept small: how our trip was, criticism of airline food and no legroom, and a raised, suspicious eyebrow when I joked about Lane's reaction to being in the first-class section. The other eyebrow rose when I mentioned the trunk of their Honda being twice the size of my car's as we put the suitcases into it.

"You have a car in San Francisco?" Bill asked suspiciously. "Lane told me she couldn't get a parking spot there for less than a hundred dollars a month."

I swallowed my laugh just in time. Lane must have been referring to the cost of parking in 1980. In *this* century, downtown garages charged four times that.

"Right," I started. "Luckily, my apartment came with free underground parking." I'd hoped that would halt the topic.

It felt like I was speaking in an avalanche zone, except in *this* zone, volume wouldn't bring the mountain down—the wrong answer would.

"Must be a really nice building," he said. "When Laney first moved up there, she looked at some places with parking. Ridiculous prices."

"Yep. I got really lucky."

Lane saved me by slipping in between us and shoving her carry-on into the trunk and slamming it shut. "Drive fast, okay, Dad? I can't wait to get home."

I watched her change her mind as soon as she eased herself gently onto the back seat, cringing at the reminder of her encounter with the jellyfish. After the first speed bump, and Lane's painful explanation of her injury, her mom handed her the sex toy—I mean, ass pillow—and her dad slowed.

25

CARSON

Mrs. Temple—"Don't be silly, Carson. Call me Jane"—gave me a quick tour of the local attractions as we drove past them. The marina, boats, the bay—yes, we have those in San Francisco, too —downtown, the suburbs, the suburbs, the suburbs, the suburbs. And, hey look! Even more suburbs. Until we finally got to the neighborhood Lane had grown up in.

We passed the high school she'd gone to—"Go, Dolphins!"—the field where she'd played soccer until she was nine, when a broken leg ruined her lifelong dream of playing all the way till she turned ten, and the grocery store where they'd shopped for over twenty-five years.

Oh yeah, I got caught up on all the latest news—unfortunately, the customer service wasn't as good as it used to be, so Jane was considering switching to the new chain store that had opened up nearby because their produce was nicer. But she wasn't sure she could because of her loyalty to the local store. Plus, their meat was fresher.

I nodded. I made sounds of understanding and agreement. But honestly, I was scared shitless. Bill and Jane were perfectly lovely people, living in a perfectly lovely suburb of a perfectly lovely town. But *holy fuck* did I hope this wasn't what Lane wanted our future to look like.

Their house was almost dead-on how I'd imagined it. Plus, back home, Lane had a dozen or so huge scrapbooks filled with pictures, ticket stubs, and random kid crap. Adorable Lane as a pigtailed little girl straddling a Barbie bike with training wheels on the sidewalk in front of the house. Studious Lane in her bedroom, looking up from a pre-teen romance novel with a smile that showed off her braces. Grumpy Lane standing in front of a Christmas tree that took up the entire living room, her awkward adolescent posture barely hinting at how beautiful she'd be a few years later. Embarrassed Lane, wearing the least flattering prom dress known to man, standing in a group of happy teens and next to the lucky idiot who was the first guy to ever put his lips on hers.

Now I was here, right where all that stuff had actually happened. An endless supply of things to tease her about.

"Make yourself at home, Carson," Jane said.

Home. Sure. All I could think about was how different it was from where I'd grown up. It was warm and lived-in, as opposed to the Bennett's sanitized house that was more showpiece than home, perpetually ready for the next magazine article or cocktail party.

"Get the Champagne glasses?" Jane asked her husband.

He took four flutes from an oak display case and set them down on the coffee table. When Jane returned from the kitchen, Bill sat on the worn blue recliner. I took the off-white couch across from him. Lane eased her ass down onto the pillow I'd put down next to me.

"Thank you." Wishing they'd offered something stronger, I

took the glass and watched the bubbles escape. "It was a long flight."

"I'm sure. We promise not to keep you up too late." Smiling, Jane held up her glass. "To family."

"To family," we all repeated.

I should've known something was off, since the liquid was darker than any Champagne I'd ever seen before, but it wasn't until I took a sip that I realized how off it was.

"Sparkling cider," Lane whispered to me as I tried to keep the disappointment off my face.

Damn. Should've known. It was going to be a long couple of days.

Grilling is great for meat and whatever hot dogs are made of. Delicious. Fun. Makes you feel like a man. But the grilling *I* went through was far less pleasant and way more emasculating. It took every ounce of concentration both Lane and I had to dodge all the questions I didn't want to answer. They were normal things parents wanted to know about their daughter's boyfriend, I'd guess. Where I grew up—San Francisco—if I had siblings—one and a half—what my career goals were—um... to never have a career goal?

I loved my life, was proud of it, even. I had Lane, the foundation, and no worries about where my next paycheck would come from. But until Lane came clean about who I was and how we'd actually gotten together, most of our reality was off limits. Thankfully they didn't ask about our love life, so Lane's virginity wasn't in question. But she hadn't even told them we were shacking up.

So we redirected the conversation to her art work about sixteen different times. She told them about her upcoming project and a little of what had inspired its theme. But even that story had holes in it.

Lane had designed the installation for the building's lobby as a reflection of her life.

"Each table is shaped like a lily pad," she explained anxiously. "Symbols of each step on the journey leading up to the infinity fountain at the far end of the lobby, which represents the future. Get it?"

They nodded either out of support or politeness, but it sure wasn't understanding.

The big piece she'd left out was that each step on the journey was actually symbolic of every guy she'd dated, every man she'd *thought* she had a future with, every asshole who'd turned out to be a frog.

"Well, it's getting late," Bill said. "I'm sure you two are exhausted. We can talk more in the morning."

It was eight-thirty. I hadn't gone to sleep at eight-thirty since I was ten, if then. But I *was* tired, and I definitely needed a break from their well-intentioned interrogation, so I was perfectly happy with my new bedtime.

My new bed*room* was less satisfactory. There was no tongue in my goodnight kiss. No sexy brunette waiting for me under the covers. No cute little ass rubbing up against my cock as I fell asleep.

Yep, it was going to be a long couple of days.

26

CARSON

I REACHED over to Lane's side of the bed and squeezed. But her ass wasn't there. In fact, none of her was there.

"Damn it, woman," I grumbled. At least I could smell coffee. That almost got her off the hook.

Wait a second. When my eyes popped open, I saw the puffy, light blue blanket, the over-fluffed pillows, and a dainty dresser with little swirls engraved into the whitewashed wood.

Oh crap, I was still in Kansas. Or the Southern California equivalent of it, at least. The only things not nauseatingly homey were a few pieces of Lane's artwork hanging on the walls. She'd told me once that she hadn't painted since high school. And, while I'd never say it out loud, at least while I was sober, there was a good reason for that. My woman was a great artist, but her talents with manipulating and cutting wood into different shapes and putting varnishes on them hadn't translated into painting. Unless she'd done the walls—nice lines, no smudges.

When I rolled onto my back, the edge of the fairytale book I'd fallen asleep reading last night poked me. All those portrayals of helpless women waiting around for a prince to show up was the best sleep aid I'd ever tried. No wonder mothers read them to kids before bed. Not *my* mother, but I was pretty sure all the others did.

How ironic that the cover of all those happy endings was currently poking *my* end. I pulled the children's book out from under my ass, hoping I hadn't just blown any good karma I'd accumulated in the past year with Lane. I really needed to keep track of that stuff better.

With my eyes mostly open, I climbed out of bed and went to look for her. She wasn't in her room, so I wandered down the hallway toward the smell of coffee. The art in the hall was a lot better. Nothing like the cold, impressionistic crap hanging on the walls of my childhood hell. This stuff had heart—lots of landscapes that didn't exist in California, flowers that didn't grow here. All signed with the same squiggle. If I'd had caffeine in my system, I might have been able to identify it.

I'd never actually cared about art before meeting Lane, but ever since she moved into my place, I'd been forced to learn about it. Our place was littered with big picture books and biographies of artists. Again, didn't really care, but human beings are capable of all sorts of odd behavior when their significant other is watching reality television.

The voices got louder as I neared the kitchen. I considered stopping and listening to what they were saying, but if it was anything about me, I was better off not knowing. I pushed open the door and saw Lane sitting at the small table and her mom at the stove, laying strips of bacon into a cast iron pan. Is there anything better than the sound of that sizzle and the smell of fresh coffee? *Besides* the sound of Lane when she comes and the scent of great sex, obviously. Ain't nothing better than that.

"Morning," I managed, rubbing my eyes and blinking.

"Good morning," her mom said, turning around to face me. That's when her expression changed, her eyes lowered, and I heard Lane gasp.

"Carson?" Lane asked somewhat calmly. "Where are your pants?"

Oh, shit. I used both hands to cover my crotch and then looked down at myself.

Could've been worse, but not by a lot. At home, I slept naked and never put anything on until after my first cup of coffee and a hot shower. I think we were all pretty relieved I'd opted to at least keep my boxer briefs on last night.

I'd decided it would've been weird to roll around in someone else's bed with my junk out. Turned out, it was also pretty damn weird to wander around someone else's house in my underwear.

"Sorry," I mumbled, backing out of the room.

"He's not a morning person. I'll be right back." Lane followed me to my room, shutting the door almost all the way. When I noticed it, she explained, "I'm not allowed to close the door if a guy is over. So they can hear what's going on."

"Damn, I never would've guessed Bill and Jane were into that kind of thing."

"Eww." She sighed. "It's so they know I'm *not* doing anything, perv." She tossed me a pair of pants. "Just be glad my dad's not home. He would've flipped."

"Because your mom was staring at my package?" I smirked.

"She was not!"

"Oh yeah she was. Couldn't take her eyes off me. Don't worry —I think she approves."

"Gross. This is going to be the longest two days of my life. Can you please at least *pretend* to be normal?"

"Maybe." I shrugged. "If I knew how."

"Okay, we should've set some ground rules. Better late than after my dad sees you half naked." She made my bed as she spoke. "Pants are to be worn at all times. Sex should never be mentioned, not even as a joke."

When she bent over to fluff a pillow or something, I came up behind her, pressing my cock to her ass.

"Careful! It still hurts a little. Plus, look but don't touch, remember? In fact, don't even look while my parents are around." She pushed me back, holding a pillow between us. "And no groping."

"Rules suck."

"I'm serious, Carson."

"Fine. Can I at least kiss you good morning?"

"No tongue."

I wasn't sure I *could* kiss her without tongue. "Can we go home now?"

"This was your idea, remember? So, no. You can handle two and a half days of celibacy.

"Yeah, but not by choice," I whined. Obviously I'd survived periodic dry patches. Just not since I met her. "Fine. I'll be on my best behavior. Treat you like you're my sister. Except not like *Anna*, more like a stepsister I want to get naked and sweaty with." I made my eyebrows bounce up and down. "What do you say, sis? Wanna get all taboo with me?"

She smacked me playfully and ran for the door. "Come on, bro. Let's get you some coffee. My dad wants to take you fishing tonight."

"Fishing? Is that a euphemism for killing me and dumping my lifeless body into the ocean?"

"I wish." Her laugh echoed through the hallway as we headed back to the kitchen.

27

CARSON

"DID YOU DO THESE?" I asked Lane, gesturing to the paintings in the hallway.

"Nope. My mom did. She's the one who got me into art. I painted the ones in your room though."

"Thought so. They're..." I squinted, looking for a word that wouldn't get me in trouble.

"Jerk," she muttered.

Now mostly dressed—I figured her mom wouldn't mind a little flash of ankle—I followed Lane back into the kitchen.

Jane had set out two plates. The appropriately-filled one was in front of the chair Lane had been sitting in. The other was across from her, piled high with all the breakfast items a lumberjack needs before a week of work. What looked like a half-dozen scrambled eggs, four full slices of bacon, two sausage mini-dicks, and two flapjacks. I was pretty sure *flapjack* was the lumberjack word for pancakes.

I remembered Lane telling me her parents had been high school sweethearts in a small town somewhere back east. She hadn't specifically mentioned it was a logging town, but the proof was sitting on the plate in front of me.

The scoop—no joke, it was an actual scoop—of butter had started to melt on top of the flapjacks, telling me that *Jane* had actually heated up the pint of syrup before she'd poured it over them.

"Sit down and eat before it gets cold," she said, leaning against the counter and sipping a cup of tea.

"Is all that for me?" Maybe she was hoping the cholesterol would kill me. Or that I'd balloon up to seven hundred pounds in the next two days, and Lane wouldn't want me anymore.

"Geez, Mom. Why'd you give him so much food?"

"He's a man," she replied as if that were answer enough.

"Yeah, *a* man. Not ten men. Dad doesn't eat like this, does he?"

Her mom paused. "I don't get a chance to cook very much anymore. I may have gone a little overboard." She poured me a cup of coffee and set it down next to my heart attack platter. "You don't have to eat it all, Carson."

One bite was more food than I usually had for breakfast. "These eggs are delicious. Thank you."

"What can I say?" Her smile was huge. "I'm a mom. I just wanted you to feel at home."

"Then you should've just tossed a cold pop-tart at me." I smiled back at her. "My mom's specialty." On the one day a week she got up early enough for breakfast.

"Your mom didn't cook?"

"My mom didn't mom."

"Oh." She tilted her head and looked concerned. "Did she work a lot?"

I shook my head while I finished chewing.

"Renee is... different," Lane answered for me. Although, I would've used a much harsher word to describe her. "Carson's family isn't as close as we are." *Definitely* would've used a harsher word to describe our family dynamics.

"We don't get along much at all, actually," I added unhelp-fully. Jane looked more confused than ever, so I tried to swing the conversation around. "Not like you guys do. Lane talks about how great you are all the time. She forgot to mention you're also an artist, though. Now I know where she got her beauty *and* her talent."

Jane stared at me in silence for a minute. Fuck, I'd always thought I was pretty good at reading women's expressions. But mothers didn't count as women, or at least, they didn't make the same kind of expressions other women did. And now that it was actually important, all I could think of was a book I was supposed to have read in high school but didn't. Flashback to the feeling of standing in front of a classroom of giggling kids and a pissed-off teacher, trying to explain why the damn grapes were so angry.

"Was that laying it on too thick?" I asked solemnly.

She looked away briefly, and Lane sighed.

"I'm not an artist," Jane said quietly. "It's just something I did for a time."

"What do you mean, Mom? A person who makes art is an artist. By definition."

"Those aren't art. Anyway, I don't do it anymore so it doesn't matter."

"Ever?" Lane's voice held such shock, I knew something was up.

"Your father and church keep me too busy nowadays." She busied herself by replacing the single sip of coffee Lane and I had taken from our cups. "So, Carson, tell me more about your family."

"Mom!"

She cut her daughter off with a raised hand. "Enough, Laney. I want to know more about Carson. He's much more interesting than I am."

And here I was trying to be subtle when changing the subject. But the last thing I needed was to be stuck in the middle of a mother-daughter argument, so I sucked it up and told Jane about my family.

"My family? Sure... um..." Sticking to the positive left me with very few things to share. "My older brother and I get along really well now."

"That's nice. You didn't get along when you were children?"

Damn it, why hadn't I left out that last word? "We did, but... um... we had a pretty tough childhood."

Obviously, my description didn't translate naturally. Thankfully, Lane provided the explanation—No, I didn't grow up in poverty. I wasn't in a gang or arrested for drinking behind the liquor store either.

Lane left the other stuff out. Stuff like, yes, after my bastard-father croaked, my mom went through a slew of men who treated her just as cruelly as my dad had. And, yeah, I'd had a few run-ins with the law for stupid rich-kid crimes like truancy and drinking high-end booze behind my private school. Nothing that ended up on my permanent record, though—records were for people whose parents didn't have lawyers on retainer.

But since I knew how important Lane's parents were to her, they were also important to me. I needed them to like me, to approve in a way my own parents never had. In a way, I'd never really *cared* if my parents had.

I'd been the one to start this whole thing. I'd called her folks and changed the plane tickets. I'd wanted this to happen, so it was now my unfortunate job to make it work. And if that meant I had to talk about my family, I'd suffer through it.

"My father passed away when I was young, and my mother lives in Los Angeles, so I don't see her often." Thankfully. "I have a stepsister who's..." My glance at Lane for advice didn't pan out. She was in wide-eyed shock, probably wondering why I was choosing to talk about my family at all. "Anna fundraises for the charity now, so I see her regularly." Pretend that was a good thing. "My brother Hayden and his new wife live in San Francisco, too. We've definitely grown closer, and a lot of that is because of your daughter's influence. They're big fans of hers."

Jane smiled at me, then Lane, then me again. See? I could do this.

"She's definitely taught me a lot about family, and a lot of other things. I'm very lucky to have her in my life."

Lane's shock had warmed into something better. Pride, maybe? Or maybe it was relief.

28

LANEY

I FELT a little bad about letting my dad take Carson off without me. Not nearly as nervous as I was about not being able to monitor Carson's every word, but he'd be fine. Probably. I just didn't see a way around it.

Who knew? Maybe they wouldn't even do much talking. Maybe they'd just sniff and growl at each other a little, silently determining dominance, like males of every other species did.

Carson was as alpha as they came, but he'd accept an older alpha. That was a thing, right? An older alpha? I wished I were more of a dog person. And understood men better.

With them gone for at least a couple hours, I had a chance to talk to my mom alone. I was worried about her. She looked older, more tired, more... not the woman I remembered. Her smile was still there, like always, but it didn't reach her eyes. Looked more like the exhausted smile she wore after a full day of serving cake and coffee and listening to church parishioners whine about their lives.

I found her reading in the living room and sat right next to her on the couch. She set down her book and wiped a lock of hair off my forehead.

"You need a trim."

"Stop." I brushed her hand away. "If I want bangs that fall into my eyes, I can have bangs that fall into my eyes." I didn't though. She was totally right—I needed a trim. "I'm not a little girl anymore, Mom."

"Don't I know it." She sighed. "So this boy makes you happy?"

"Yes, but..." That wasn't what I wanted to talk to her about.

She turned toward me and took my hand in hers. "But what, honey? You can tell me. Something about Carson?"

Great. Now she was worried about me. "No. Carson's amazing. He is. I have nothing to complain about."

She smiled. "I can't tell you how happy hearing that makes me, Laney. It really does."

Why had I ever worried about my parents hating him? I couldn't believe I'd waited this long to have them meet. Crap, when I thought of all the time I wasted worrying about it...

"He's not the kind of man I thought you'd end up with, of course. Carson is so much less..." When her brow came together as she searched for a word, all the guilt I'd felt for waiting so long suddenly seemed like the best use of time ever. What horrible word was she going to say?

"Boring."

Wait. What? "Did you just say you expected me to end up with someone boring?"

She stared at me for a moment. "If Carson makes you happy, that's all that matters."

"I guess so," I said warily, wondering if I wanted to know why she thought I'd choose to be with someone boring. Then I remembered I *had* been with someone boring. A few someones boring, actually. Every jackass before Carson.

"You're right—he's definitely not boring. He's funny and

sweet and supportive of what I want to do. Not to mention that he puts up with me, which, as you know, isn't always easy."

"You forgot to mention he's not too bad to look at."

"Mom! Gross!" I said, laughing with her. "Yeah, he's not too bad to look at either. Honestly, I didn't even know men could be so great—except Dad, of course, but you know..."

Her smile faded. "Yes, I know."

"Mom?" I started, not knowing what I was going to say next. "I'm glad the men are out because I wanted to talk to you privately."

"Uh-oh. If it's not Carson..."

I shook my head again. "I wanted to talk to you... about *you*."

"Me?"

The amount of surprise encompassed in that one word felt like a lifetime of guilt slamming down on me.

My mom was incredible—giving, kind, supportive, helpful, and a great listener. Sadly, all of that meant I could almost guarantee no one had ever wondered how she was feeling—including her. She was a rock, there for anyone and everyone who needed her. But who'd been there for *her*? Not me, that's for sure.

"How are you? Really?"

"I'm..." She paused for a breath. "I'm busy. We started a new support group at the church for women and mothers, and it's going wonderfully. Some of their stories are difficult to hear, but it's important for them to have a safe place to talk." She continued, telling me a few horror stories of abuse or neglect, along with a few happier ones like women finding jobs that paid enough to support their kids.

And while I could tell my mom was proud of them and the hard work they were doing to reach their goals, I wondered if she'd ever shared her own story with the women. Sadder still—

in a purely narcissistic way, mind you—was the jealousy I felt flare up at the idea she might've shared something with *them* that she'd never shared with me.

She was amazing, and brilliant, and had it all together, and nothing could ever change how much I loved her. But realistically, how much time had I ever spent actually getting to know her?

"That's awesome, Mom. I'm sure they really appreciate it. But how are you besides busy?"

She looked at me silently for a minute, maybe weighing how honest she could be.

"Are you happy?" I prompted.

She took a deep breath. "I'm always happy to be of service to others."

I cringed. "Geez, Mom. I know that. And it's great. But I want to know if you are happy when you're not doing things for other people. When you're here with Dad or by yourself."

"I don't know." Three of the most common words in the English language that, most of the time, held no meaning. But when she said them, they were full of fear, confusion, and regret. "I don't know anymore, Laney."

I waited for her to continue.

It took her a while, but eventually, she did. "I have so much—it feels wrong to want more." She straightened out the bottom edge of my t-shirt until I brushed her hand away.

"That's not wrong, Mom. That's normal. We all deserve to be happy. You don't think less of those women because they want that for themselves, do you?"

She shook her head. "Of course, not."

She must have been a little selfish at some point. All young people were. I just didn't know how to help her think that way again.

I glanced around the room, hoping something would trigger a good idea. But it was all the same crap that—

Crap.

I'd almost kicked Carson out on the street this morning because he'd come very close to suggesting the paintings I'd done were crap. Fortunately for him, he'd stopped talking at exactly the right moment.

My mom had always been the painter in the family, but the stuff hanging on the walls now wasn't hers. I couldn't remember a time growing up when she wasn't painting or sculpting something. Taking down one painting and putting another up, or reorganizing a space so there'd be room for her latest sculpture.

Looking back, I guess she'd stopped while I was a teenager, but I'd been too selfish and preoccupied to really care. She'd been my biggest supporter, had taught me about form and perspective, had signed me up for my first wood carving course, and bought me my first set of chisels.

And now, the artwork on the walls was somebody else's, and picture frames had replaced the carved figures that used to take up every horizontal surface.

"Where's all of your artwork, Mom?"

She had taught me how to love art as much as she taught me how to love myself and my family. I knew how impossible it would be for me to stop creating it, and it couldn't have been much different for her.

"It was taking up too much room, and I like having pictures of our family where I can see them all the time. They're good memories."

I nodded. Because I agreed, and also because I understood. She missed me. She missed the family we used to be, the people we used to be.

"Darn it." She patted my leg and stood up before I could stop her. "I need to go shopping before the boys get back with the catch of the day." She grabbed her bag, keys, and sunglasses and headed through the door.

"Mom!" I called after her. "Can we talk more?"

"Later? Of course we can."

Of course we could. But *would* we?

29

CARSON

As Bill and I drove toward what might soon be my watery grave, I stared at the profile of the man Lane had put on a pedestal when she was a little girl. Seemed like a pretty solid pedestal too, since he was still up there.

Honestly, it looked like a fairly normal middle-aged guy profile, nothing remarkable or heroic about it. Bill was just a man. A good man, but still just a man. And all men got stupid when it came to women. I'd guess that went double when it came to their daughters. Hopefully I'd never know for sure. Not because I didn't want to have kids—I definitely did. I just didn't want *girl* kids. Because I'd know what the *boy* kids were thinking when they looked at my girl kid. Perverted little pricks.

Must be hell having a daughter.

When he nodded, I realized I'd said it aloud. "You have no idea."

"You did a great job, though. Lane is an amazing woman, and you're not in prison."

"Only because I know how to hide a body."

He was joking, right? I let out my breath when he turned and I could see his smile.

"Laney said you have a sense of humor, Carson. So where is it?"

"I left it in my other pants." The clean ones. "To be honest, sir, I've never done a meet-the-parents thing before."

"Never? You're what? Twenty-five? And you've never met a girl's parents before? What's wrong with you?"

I glanced at my watch. "How long you got?"

He chuckled briefly, keeping his eyes on the road. "So you're the type who never gets serious about anyone?"

"I used to think so. Now I know I'm the type who only gets serious about the *right* one. I figured that out the day I met your daughter. Haven't doubted it a single moment since." Except when she forced me to watch the first few episodes of *Sex and the City*. That was almost a deal-breaker. Talk about a misleading title. I couldn't be the only one who assumed it was soft porn, could I?

"How serious is this relationship?"

Ugh. Here we go. The unavoidable conversation I'd never be ready for. "Serious enough that I want to marry her."

"Are you saying that because you think it's what I want to hear?"

"Not at all. If I said what I think you want to hear, it would've been something like: 'Your daughter is too good for a bum like me. I'm going to go crawl under a rock so she can find someone better.'"

He chuckled again. "Sounds about right. Nothing personal, though. You seem like a nice fella."

Huh. I'd been called a lot of things, but "nice fella" wasn't one of them. Neither were either of those words separately.

"That said, I don't know if I'll ever believe *any* man is good enough for my daughter."

"Me neither. But I'd like to be. Which is why..." Deep breath. Don't make eye contact. Hold onto something secure, just in case he decides to toss me out of the moving car. "I want to marry her. Soon."

The only sound I heard for a minute was the pounding of my heart. Finally, about three thousand beats later, he spoke.

"Why?"

"Um..." *Why* was I clutching onto the armrest? *Why* was my heart pounding loud enough for him to hear? *Why* was this man's approval so damn important to me? All good questions.

"I asked you a question, son. Why do you want to marry my daughter?"

"I heard you, sir. I'm just wondering why you asked. I mean, if you know your daughter at all—which you obviously do—you already know why. It makes more sense to ask every other man she's ever met why they *wouldn't*."

"Alright, then. Why do you think they wouldn't?"

I understood his intent immediately—the sneaky bastard. This was like in those job interviews, when they asked what your worst quality was. And everyone always says, "perfection-ism," which, for the interviewer, translates to: I'm a big, fat liar. They'd heard it fourteen billion times and had never, ever believed it.

"My guess is you want me to tell you what I think is wrong with your daughter. Then you expect me to lie about it and say something I think you want to hear." Which would be the smart thing to do. Unfortunately... "I don't do that, Bill. I don't lie to your daughter, and I won't lie to you. I'm going to try to answer your question honestly."

"That's fair."

Fair? Not even a little. None of this conversation was fair. Any interaction between a father and his daughter's lover was innately unfair. If it were fair, I wouldn't be sweating this badly.

I cleared my throat. "None of those men wanted to marry Lane as much as I do because she didn't *let* them. Because she never found someone to trust and love enough to be herself, to show them who she really is. For some crazy, I'll-never-understand reason, she decided to show me. I'm not particularly special and, to be honest, she *could* probably do better than me, at least on paper."

This wasn't getting any easier. "But your daughter chose *me*. She loves *me*. Enough to open herself up and not be afraid I would judge the parts of her that she *doesn't* like. And, at least in that, she's right. I won't judge her, and I will love all of her. Even the less-than-perfect parts." Like her obsession with *Sex and the City*. "Believe me, I know how lucky that makes me. And as implausible as we seem, I know how good we are for each other."

Bill was quiet for a while, long enough to make me worry. "Jane and I barely knew each other when we got married. Made sense—we barely knew ourselves. So I never felt what you feel about my daughter. I still don't think I know my wife that well. We had a good life together, didn't fight, were close. But we didn't grow together—we didn't even grow apart. I think we just grew *up*. Unfortunately, only then did we understand we were never really meant to be together to begin with. I'm glad my daughter found someone who understands her."

"Thanks." Then it hit me. "Wait. Go back a second. What do you mean you were never meant to be together?" That went against everything I knew about Lane's parents, everything Lane had told me, everything she believed.

Bill and Jane had the picture-perfect happily ever after. They had the relationship Lane had always been searching for, the kind she wanted *us* to have.

He sighed. "Laney doesn't know. We'd planned to tell her eventually but..."

"Please don't tell me you're splitting up, Bill." Every muscle in my body cramped, and every cell screamed, "No!" This would hurt her so much. "Please don't."

"No."

Thank God.

"But things seem to be moving in that direction."

I leaned on the dashboard for balance. "So you're, what, just pretending to still live at the house? For Lane's benefit?"

"Hold up, son," he said, with his voice and a hand. "I still live in the house."

"Oh, okay." I'd never been happier to have misunderstood something.

"I'm pretending to sleep in a marital bed for Laney's benefit."

Oh, shit.

"For the last few months I've been sleeping in the guest room. We've been putting off the inevitable conversation, mostly so we don't hurt Laney. That's why Jane suggested you stay for a few days. I'm sure you being here when we tell her will help her get through it."

Why the fuck would he think that? Obviously, I had no issues with divorce. My mother had gone through enough of them, and Hayden did it when he met Andi.

But the news that Lane's parents were going to split up and were planning to tell her *now* completely screwed up all of the romantic proposal plans I hadn't made yet.

Lane would not take this news well. Maybe I could fake an emergency back home and get her out of here before they had a chance to tell her.

"I think I'm gonna be sick."

"I just got the upholstery cleaned, damn it!" Bill yanked the car to the shoulder of the road and knocked it into park, reaching across me to open my door.

I'd been speaking metaphorically. But as soon as the door opened, I can't say the idea of jumping out and running for the bushes didn't cross my mind. I finally understood why they were called *freeways*—the side of a road had never looked this much like freedom to me before.

In ten seconds, I could be across the dead grass and over that stone wall, terrifying the family whose backyard I landed in.

I couldn't run. Not from this. Definitely not from Lane. When I'd made a commitment to her, my family had become her family just like Bill and Jane were *my* family, along with all the baggage and issues families carried along with them.

Holy fuck, did I have a lot of other people's shit to deal with now.

"Your upholstery's safe, Bill. But we have a problem to fix. And yeah, I mean *we*. And yeah, it's going to involve a lot more talking than either of us is comfortable with."

30

CARSON

WE NEVER MADE it to the boat, so any plan Bill might have had for tossing me overboard was ruined. My nausea comment in the car might've made him think I couldn't control my gag reflex. Instead, the poor guy had to actually listen to all the verbal vomit I spewed, as if I knew what the hell I was talking about. So, yeah, we talked—openly and honestly. But, to prove we were still men, we didn't look at each other even once.

"That the best you got?" Bill asked. No, the question wasn't directed at me. At least I hoped it wasn't.

"It's Chilean Sea Bass, and we're standing on a dock in California," the fishmonger at the little shop on the pier said flatly. "If you wanted something fresh, then no, it's not the best thing we got."

"Why are you selling it, then?"

The guy shrugged. "Tourists. They watch too many cooking shows and think 'California Cuisine' only includes Chilean Sea Bass, avocados, and granola. We got those too, if you want 'em."

Bill sighed deeply as if it were one of his last breaths. "I need something local. Give me two of them. Biggest ones." He pointed to another chunk of fish, one that had its head still attached.

I stared into the poor bastard's dead eye and swore to never eat fish again. If I hadn't talked Bill out of the whole boat-bonding thing, that could've been me.

"How am I supposed to convince my wife I went fishing in the bay if I bring home something Chilean?" he muttered.

The truth hit me when we were waiting for our "catch" to be wrapped in paper and rung up. What? We had to bring home something, or the women would know we hadn't been fishing. Normally, I would've just gone with the we-went-to-a-strip-club-instead excuse, but it didn't seem right with Lane's dad. Plus Lane never believed it anyway.

"Got a question for you, Bill. When's the last time you really talked with your wife?"

"I talk to her every day."

"Not talk *to*. Talk *with*. Completely different. When's the last time you had an honest conversation about what you both want from life?"

He scratched his chin. "Only young people ask that kind of question."

I grabbed the fish, thanked the guy behind the counter, and walked to the register. "No offense, but that's the dumbest thing I've ever heard, Bill. Unless you are on your deathbed or are one of the nonexistent people who actually have everything they want in every way, you should be asking yourself that question. People are either living or waiting to die. I could be wrong—it's happened once or twice—but you don't seem like the waiting-to-die type to me."

He seemed more like the type who was about to smack me. It had happened a lot more than once or twice.

"Am I wrong about you, Bill?"

He glared at me for another moment. I took the opportunity to slide my credit card from my wallet and set it on the counter next to our big catch. He nabbed the card and gave it back to me, reaching for his own wallet.

"We gonna fight about this?" I asked, shoving my card at the cashier before he could.

"My daughter is an artist living in one of the most expensive cities in the country. Keep your money and use it to take her out once in a while. For something better than a burger."

"She really hasn't told you anything about me, has she?"

He froze in place, thinking about something I wasn't privy to long enough for the cashier to swipe my card and hand me a receipt to sign.

Shit. How badly did I offend him? And why? And what should I do now? "You okay, Bill?" If this trip ended with me putting Lane's dad into the hospital over a stupid comment, she'd never forgive me. I glanced at his heart, then his left arm. If anything on television was real, I knew the signs of a heart attack.

I dropped the pen and reached for him, just in case he fell over. "Bill, you still with me? Say something."

He blinked. Then again. But I'd need words before I felt safe.

"Nothing."

"No, something. Say *something*. I need to know you're okay."

"She doesn't talk to me."

How bad is it to be thankful someone is *only* having a nervous breakdown?

"Who you talking about, Bill?"

"Laney. Jane. My daughter didn't tell me anything about you. What I know I know because she told her mother. And that's just about all Jane ever says to me—what Laney's doing. My wife and daughter don't talk to me because I don't listen. Because I..." His eyes glistened with the realization, and then he looked straight at me and silently asked for help. "What if it's too late?"

In a moment neither of us would ever forget or mention to another living soul, we connected.

"It's going to be okay, sir. Let's go home and make it right."

31

LANEY

MY MOM ASKED me to watch the rice so she could wrap the fish in foil and put it in the oven. I'm not sure why the rice needed watching. I think she just wanted me to keep her company and didn't trust me with anything more complicated.

The *men folk* were "resting"—i.e., having a beer. Evidently, they'd expended a lot of energy pulling two dying fish out of the water and needed a break. After my mom was done prepping, and the rice no longer needed a babysitter, she suggested we go sit down with the men until it was all ready.

They stopped talking as soon as we came into the living room, which made me a little nervous. I sat next to Carson on the couch, and my mom took the chair across from my dad's. They looked at each other, something passing between them that made my mom sit up a little straighter and take a deep breath.

I knew it. My dad hated my boyfriend. Carson's normal charisma had failed, and now my parents were going to give me the we-don't-approve talk. Then my mom and I would start crying, I'd start yelling at them for being so judgmental, and we'd spend the next twenty-four hours not speaking to each other. Maybe Carson could switch our plane tickets again—get us both out of here sooner.

"Laney, we need to talk." Dad set his drink down on the coffee table, and I steeled myself for the impending argument. "I'm just going to come out and say it. Your mom and I have been having some problems for a while now and were headed toward a separation."

Carson's "what" was even louder than mine, but that wasn't saying much considering how hard my throat had just clamped down.

They were headed toward a separation? What did that even mean? "You're splitting up?"

"For future reference, sir," Carson said. "That wasn't a great way to come out and say it."

I looked at him, eyes and mouth gaping. "You knew? You knew about this, and you didn't fucking tell me?"

"Language, Laney!" my mom sputtered.

"Right, Mom. Me using a bad word is really the shit we should be focusing on right now."

Carson looked at me.

My dad looked at me.

My mom looked at me.

And I broke.

My eyes stung, and my lungs couldn't fill with air. I looked around desperately before realizing that, for once, I couldn't go to my parents for help. They wouldn't be there for much longer.

"Laney," my mom said softly, "wait. Let us explain."

Explain what? My parents were in love and then they weren't. Pretty sure that summed it up, didn't it? Oh, except for the added bonus that the three of them had all been very careful not to tell me what was going on in my own family.

Without saying anything, I ran. I was halfway down the hall before realizing I didn't want to be in the room I'd grown up in, the one where I'd dreamt of having the kind of relationship my parents had. Pretending I couldn't hear sounds no kid ever wants to hear coming from their parents' room.

I didn't want to be in the house where every day I came home and tossed my backpack onto the fourth kitchen chair and pulled out my homework while my mom cooked and my dad helped me. Except when I was doing math.

I didn't look at them as I went through the living room and out the front door, slamming it behind me without waiting to see if it actually closed or not. I jogged down the street, following the path I'd taken every day from kindergarten until high school. But this time, I didn't know where I was going. How could something so pure, so comfortable and safe, suddenly feel so unrecognizable?

I didn't want to be here. I didn't want this to be happening. I didn't even want Carson to be near me. Because, suddenly, I wasn't sure people were meant to be together. Maybe it was psychologically impossible.

"Bill, Jane," I heard Carson yell and the door fly open and bang against the siding. "Start talking. Now!"

What was there to talk about? People grew and changed and decided they didn't like each other anymore. And there was no way to stop it from happening. An inevitability.

"Lane! Lane! Damn it. Slow down."

"I just want to be alone for a little while," I said without turning.

"No, you don't. You want to hide and start thinking all sorts of unhealthy shit, and I'm not going to let you."

I didn't stop. Or look back. I couldn't.

"I'll tackle you if I have to, but I'd really rather not," he said, easily catching up to me. "At least not until we get home, and I have a much better reason to. Don't force me to do it, Lane. You know I will."

I shrugged his hand off my shoulder.

"Come on, babe. Think of the neighborhood kids. Lots of permanent scarring would happen if I had you on the ground underneath me right now."

I knew how awful I looked as soon as I saw his expression. Pity maybe? I didn't know... anything anymore.

"Stop running away." He spun in front of me and held both my shoulders. Then his hand moved to my face, my cheeks, gently wiping away my tears. "Why didn't you let them explain?"

"Because I don't need to hear why, after twenty-eight years of marriage, they're giving up." Then I told him what I feared the most. "Why would it be different for anyone else, Carson?"

"Don't do this, Lane." His eyes intensified, his jaw clenched, his grip on my arms tightened. "Please don't do this."

"I'm not breaking up with you. I just... Would you ever give up on me, Carson?"

"You? No, never. Do you have any idea what I went through to *get* you?"

"Yeah, it was hell," I teased. "All those innuendos and obvious hints? You poor thing."

"I know. And then I had to deal with your insane libido. Still do, actually." His voice softened. "Believe me, that's something I will never, ever give up."

"Your sacrifice is remarkable." I wiped my eyes. "But what about the rest? Like when we fight? We're *going* to fight, and we suck at it."

He stared at me for a minute, long enough for me to understand where his head was. He had the same faraway expression every time he thought about his father.

"I've seen fights," he said. "I've been in fights. But I've never known someone so completely that I could ignore anything they say."

"You consider that a good thing?"

He nodded. "If you ever say something to be hurtful, then I'd know *you're* hurting. You're a beautiful person, babe, so when you're not, I know something else is going on, something deeper. And, after some poor reaction time, I *remember* I know that and try to figure out what's really going on.

"That's why I've never worried about us fighting. Yeah, it'll happen. But ultimately, I know you don't really want to hurt me. Just like I never want to hurt you. So as long as we don't forget that, five minutes of yelling at each other now and then won't change how much I love you."

"You're a good man, Carson Bennett."

"Plus, I've mapped out a contingency plan for every possible reason you might want to get rid of me, and why I might wanna get rid of you. Your list of reasons is a lot longer. Mine only has one."

"What's the one?"

He hesitated, looking at the ground a few feet away. "If you ever get dumped in toxic waste and become a super-villain." He stopped laughing when I smacked him in the chest. "Okay, truth?"

"No, I want you to lie to me," I grumbled.

"If you ever come to your senses and realize how much better you are than I am. If you ever decide you would be happier without me. Then I would let you go. I'd be a miserable wreck, but I'd let you go if I knew it would make you happy."

"It wouldn't."

"Then we don't have to worry about it. Right?" He paused. "Now, I think you owe it to your parents to hear them out. They're both good people who would never give up on you, right? So don't give up on them."

I nodded slowly. "I'm still mad at you for not telling me."

"In my defense, I have very little experience caring about what families think or do, and we haven't exactly had a lot of alone time to chat since I found out an hour ago. Plus, there's a lot more to the story, but you need to hear it from them. Not from me. I'm just an innocent bystander in all this. An innocent, fantastic-looking bystander."

I wasn't ready to open my mouth and smile yet, so my laugh went through my nose and tickled.

"I won't lie to you, babe." He kissed my cheeks, smacked his lips together, and said, "Salty. Like the ocean your dad and I never actually made it onto. The fish is fraudulent." He slipped the cuff of his shirt over his hand and gently wiped away the rest of my tears.

"Fish can be fraudulent?" I asked quietly, still fighting off my smile. Going to a strip club was his default excuse for everything. He never went to work or meetings or the store to pick me up my favorite ice cream. I was just lucky they happened to carry mint chocolate swirl at the local nonexistent strip club.

I might've bought the lie once or twice, but one, he's a terrible liar, two, our neighborhood would never allow a strip club to operate there and three, in San Francisco, almost all the strippers are men.

"You're going to tell me you went to a strip club instead, aren't you?"

"Sure am. Where do you think we got the fish?"

"Ugh." Instead of smacking him, I burrowed my head into his chest and squeezed him as tightly as I could, wishing I could live right there forever and never have to move again.

Unfortunately, a car would eventually come and kill us both if we didn't get out of the middle of the street.

"I'm not quite ready to talk to them yet."

"Then, come on." He pulled me away from the house. "You can show me where you scraped your knee when you were ten, or the park where you and your friends used to get loaded late at night, or the woods you had to walk through on your way to school where lots of spooky shit happened. Assuming these suburbs are anything like the suburbs in almost every supernatural movie ever made."

"If you want to see the neighborhood's haunted house"— I yanked him across the street by the hand—"it's this way."

32

LANEY

AFTER ABOUT THIRTY minutes of ruining all the myths Carson had ever heard about the suburbs, we walked back to the house. Before we opened the door, I squeezed his hand and said, "Someday you'll have to tell me what's on my list of reasons to get rid of *you*."

"And remind you of all the reasons I'm not good enough for you? Not a chance. That'd be cheating. I have my fingers crossed you won't figure it out for another fifty or sixty years."

My parents stood in the entryway, right next to each other, the same way they had the countless times I stayed out later than my curfew. But this time they didn't look angry. They looked tired. Older. Sadder.

I brushed by them and plopped myself down on the couch. "Fine. Let's hear it."

No one said anything. No truth. No lies. Nothing.

"Okay, then. I'll start," I snapped. "Since we're all coming clean and everything. Carson and I also have something to tell you that you won't like."

"You told me you didn't knock her up," my dad growled at Carson.

"I didn't, sir! At least..." He looked at me, the question in his eyes. "I didn't, did I?"

"No, I'm not pregnant. But we're living together." I left out *in sin* even though I knew that's what they were thinking.

"And...?" my mom asked.

"And we've *been* living together for a while now. In one house. Without being married."

"We know, Laney."

"How?"

"You and Hillary aren't living together anymore," she said, "and you never mentioned getting another roommate."

"I could've been living alone."

"When we call you in the morning, he's there. When we call you at night, he's there."

"You're not mad? Or... disappointed?"

My mom glanced at my dad, handing it over to him. Great. Here it came.

"Of course I was unhappy about it. But we understand the world a bit better than you give us credit for, Laney."

I nodded curtly. I mean, I was very pleasantly surprised they weren't freaking out about it. I'd been dreading this moment forever. But I was still mad at them for not telling me they were splitting up, so I couldn't let them see my relief.

And since that went so much better than expected, I figured I should come clean about the other thing I'd been holding back. "Carson's rich. Like, really rich." I opted not to use the word *filthy* because Carson had already shown them that side of himself. "Really, really rich."

In their eyes, *rich* had always been the equivalent of privileged, self-indulgent, non-charitable asshole. Exactly the kind of person they hated, if hate was something they did. But they couldn't fool me—judging people was something they only *pretended* not to do. I'd seen their side glances to each other and their polite brushoffs whenever they saw someone flaunt their wealth.

All this time I'd been afraid of their reaction to this news the most. Because of how wrong they'd be about Carson. That, even though he was filthy—rich and otherwise—he always seemed disconnected from it and never knew why anyone would flaunt it.

But they didn't react. They both just sat there, looking at me, as if they were still waiting for the ball to drop. But I'd already dropped the biggest balls there were—Carson's.

Shit. Thank goodness I didn't say that out loud.

"Well…?" I prompted, preparing for the head shaking and the disappointed sighs to start. Then the condemnation and prayers for him to become a better human being.

"Well, what?" my mom asked.

"Well, he's rolling in money."

"Not literally," he said calmly. "The bed I use for rolling around in money is back in San Francisco."

Instead of being horrified by the joke, my dad laughed. He actually laughed. Out loud. "Good for you, Carson."

"Good for him?" I echoed. "Seriously? If we're all being honest now, be honest. Tell him how you feel about rich people."

"Hon, take a breath."

"I'm breathing just fine. Thanks, *Dad*."

"I don't think they're going to take the bait," Carson whispered to me.

"What does that mean?" I snapped.

"It means," he said, more loudly since they could hear him anyway, "you're trying to pick a fight with people who aren't interested in fighting you. Must be frustrating."

I ground my teeth together. "Why are you taking their side?"

"There are no sides, babe. Everyone in this room loves you

and wants you to be happy." He tilted his head. "Except you, evidently."

I took a deep breath, not because my dad had suggested it, but to prepare myself for a biting response. To who? To Carson? No, of course not. To my parents? Whose only request was that I breathe?

Crap! He was right. It was so maddening to be ready for a fight only to not have anyone to engage with. All that adrenaline wasted. Plus, the anxiety, fear, uncertainty, and shame leading up to it.

I felt the heat that had begun as anger turn into embarrassment, blushing cheeks and everything. When Carson took my hand, I couldn't figure out how he knew that was the moment I needed him to.

"You're okay with him being rich?"

"Carson," my dad said, shifting in his seat, "did you make the money selling drugs, scamming people, or anything unsavory?"

"Not that anyone can prove, sir."

Both of them were smiling at him as if this was all a big joke.

"I hate telling people this because it gives them the wrong idea about me," Carson said calmly. "But I inherited a lot of money when my father died. After I got rid of it, I got even more of the stuff when his sister, my aunt, passed away."

I pulled my hand out of his so I could air quote something he'd said. "He 'got rid of that' by starting a foundation. What I left out was the name of the foundation. It's the Bennett Foundation, and he started it with lots of his *money*." I extended the word *money* to remind them how much they disliked talking about it.

"We know that, too."

"You do?"

"Laney, what kind of father wouldn't check out the man his little girl is shacking up with? Of course I looked him up."

"And because you're probably desperate to know," my mom said to Carson, "we also found a few articles about your... more youthful pursuits."

"I was actually desperately trying *not* to think about that, Jane. But I understand. Still hoping you didn't watch any of the videos that might be out there, but...?"

"We didn't." I'd never seen my mom's eyebrows so high, but my dad was still smiling. "We're more concerned about the man you've become, how you treat our daughter, and that you don't plan on acting like an idiot again in the future."

"I can honestly promise that I'm not planning on it." Carson squinted, hopefully not wondering if there were any videos out there of the way he treated me. We'd only videotaped ourselves once, and there was only one copy, tucked deep in my computer in a recipe folder, labeled *Spicy Sausage Fillher*. It was Carson's idea to add the *h* and leave out the space.

"Early on in our relationship," he said seriously, "I did something really stupid. I hurt her. I thought I could live without her, so I told her it was over. Thankfully, she's a lot smarter than I am and had figured out how wrong I was. I'll never make that mistake again."

Speaking of mistakes... "Did you cheat on Mom?"

"No," my dad said angrily, "of course not."

"Neither did I," my mom said after a pause. It hadn't even occurred to me she might. I'm not sure why. I guess I'm a sexist, after all. After being with as many cheaters as I had, it was the easiest answer—whether or not is was the correct answer.

I looked at Carson, maybe with guilt in my eyes, or with fear.

"We're not all pricks, Lane."

I took a deep breath. "I know." And I did. I knew Carson would never cheat. He might flirt or jokingly beg me to make out with another woman so he could watch, but he'd never hurt me like that.

I faced my mom because there was a chance—a small one—I'd understand it better coming from her than from my dad. "Why are you splitting up?"

Her mouth opened but no words came out. So, like always, my dad butted in.

"We're not."

33

LANEY

ALL THREE OF us snapped our heads in my dad's direction.

"We're not?" my mom asked at the same time I asked, "Are you *trying* to make this more confusing for me?"

My dad shook his head. "I said we were heading toward a split. But after talking through some things today, that's not the direction I want us to go." He looked at my mom. "I don't know if we'll make it, but I don't want to give up without at least trying.

"I've known you were unhappy for a long time, Jane. I was just afraid to ask why... because I didn't want to hear it was my fault. Carson helped me figure out that as afraid as I was to hear your answer, it didn't even compare to how afraid I am to lose you."

"I helped you figure all that out?" When everyone looked at him, Carson smirked and added, "Yeah, of course, I did. I do stuff like that all the time."

I sat there on mute while my dad spoke. I'm not sure I'd ever heard him talk this much before, certainly not about his feelings. My mom listened with tears in her eyes and, as much as I wanted to hug her, to make her stop feeling, I didn't. Because she needed this. Maybe even more than my dad did.

She needed to hear what was in his heart, all the things he regretted not saying, all the times he'd been so afraid of losing her that he'd shut himself off and pretended everything was fine.

My mom reached over and took his hand in hers without saying a word.

My tears started falling soon after that. To know what I'd always thought was an ideal relationship had actually been broken.

"Um..." Carson said quietly. "Lane, could I see you in the kitchen?"

I knew I should've gotten up, left my parents to sort things out on their own, but what if something went wrong? Although it wasn't as if I could keep them together just by sitting there staring at them.

But Carson was insistent, and I got the message.

"We're going to leave you two to talk privately."

They didn't even look up as I stood and let him lead me into the kitchen. As soon as we turned the corner, I smelled it.

"Oh, crap! The fish." I ran to the stove to turn the fan on high then went to open the window. Carson pulled the fire alarm off the ceiling before it started screaming.

"I didn't want to alarm anyone while you were all emoting." Smoke billowed out of the oven when Carson opened it. He waved his hand in front of his face, grabbed a pot holder. "But I'm fairly sure blackened fish isn't supposed to taste like charcoal."

"I can't believe my mom forgot. She never forgets stuff like that."

"She has more important things to focus on right now." Carson used a fork to lift the fish out of the pan and put them on a cutting board, then started scraping the charred skin away. "You okay?"

I leaned back on the counter, only vaguely realizing the jellyfish sting didn't hurt anymore. "Guess so. Might depend on what they decide, though."

"They love each other, Lane. That's obvious. But they stopped talking. People change. What we want changes. If we stop sharing who we are along the way, how's the other person supposed to know?"

"They can't?"

"Bingo." He tipped the lid of the rice to the side and peered inside before turning off the heat underneath it. "Honestly, I don't know if they'll be fine. I hope so, and I think they're both willing to try, so I have a good feeling about it. But the only thing you can do now is tell them you love them, and then let them do what they need to do."

"When did you get to be so knowledgeable about relationships?"

"This afternoon. When I thought your dad was going to murder me, I had a second to think about stuff." He chuckled and faced me. "You really want to know?" He waited for me to nod. "Because, for the last year, I've spent every waking moment thanking the universe for the one I have."

We kissed. Two lips meeting two lips. Something simple that meant so much.

We separated when we heard someone clear their throat.

"You kids mind if we skip dinner?" my dad asked. "I'd like to take your mother somewhere."

"Where?" I asked.

I regretted the question as soon as I saw the blush on my mom's cheeks. Oh God, what if he was taking her to a sex shop or something? *Please don't answer. Please don't answer. Please don't answer.*

"You want to tell them or should I?" My dad nudged her.

"We're going to the art store."

If art store had another meaning, I didn't want to know.

Thankfully, my mom clarified, and not in the way I dreaded.

"I'm going to start painting again."

"You've inspired your mother, Laney. She wants to be an artist again."

I squealed and ran to her for a hug. "That's awesome, Mom!"

She spoke into my ear. "You were right. I forgot how much I needed it. I'll never be *me* without it."

"I'm so proud of you," I whispered. When we pulled apart, I saw my dad shaking Carson's hand.

"You might want to grab something to eat while you're out," Carson was saying. "I don't think I can scrape enough charcoal off these for four of us."

"Next time you come to visit, let's plan on actually making it to the boat."

"As long as you promise to bring me back alive, you're on."

We followed them into the living room where they gathered their stuff.

"Bill?" Carson asked. "Does this mean you think I'm good enough for your daughter?"

My dad took a deep breath, pondering his answer. Just that much of a delay set us all on edge.

"Does it really matter what I think?" he asked eventually. "Okay, if you really want to know what I think, here it is..." He cleared his throat. "I never thought it was possible for anyone to want our daughter to be as happy as we do and love her as much as we do. You proved me wrong, son. You proved me wrong."

34

CARSON

AFTER LANE'S parents went out, she and I spent the rest of the evening watching repeats of *The Big Bang Theory*. It gave both of us an escape and Lane a chance to process what had gone down with her folks. As much as I wanted to press her to talk about it, I didn't.

By the time Bill and Jane got back around ten o'clock, Lane was fast asleep, her legs tucked up on the couch and her head on my lap.

"It's after ten o'clock. On a school night." I chose to go with a parental-sounding stern yet quiet tone, so I wouldn't wake up my girl. "Where have you two been?"

"The art store," Jane answered guiltily.

"Sure you were." Nobody winked, but we were all aware that art stores didn't stay open until ten. Any details beyond that, I didn't want to know.

Too bad Lane missed seeing the smiles on their faces, the way they looked at each other as they tiptoed into their bedroom...together. Okay, she was probably better off *not* seeing that part, but she'd find out tomorrow. Our flight home didn't leave until noon.

I slipped out from under her and carried her to bed. I'd have loved to bring her to my room, to know I'd wake up next to her, but that would've been against house rules. Even if her parents wouldn't care anymore, Lane would. And that was what mattered. So I carefully set her down on her bed and flipped the ends of the comforter up around her until she looked like a green and blue striped burrito.

A few minutes later, I made my way to the guest room, desperately trying not to hear any noise from her parent's room.

As soon as I got into bed, I grabbed the book of fairytales, hoping they'd put me to sleep. They did.

I woke up at nine-something, put on clothing this time, and wandered toward the voices.

Jane and Bill looked up from their breakfasts to say, "Good morning."

"Would you like some coffee?" Jane asked, scooting her chair back.

"More than world peace at the moment, yeah. But I'll get it." I took the biggest mug they had out of the cupboard.

It said, "*Often the most difficult roads lead to the most beautiful destinations.*"

And all the *other* times, they lead to cliffs, or bars, or bad decision making.

"Where's Lane?"

"She's in her room on the phone, just like when she was a teenager. You know her friend Hillary, don't you?"

"Yep." Better than I wished I did. I peeked under the Tupperware cloche covering a plate on the counter. Two slices of bacon, scrambled eggs, and a slice of toast. "Is this spoken for?"

Jane shook her head. "It's all yours. I learned my lesson yesterday, but if it's not enough—"

"It's perfect. You're a great mom." I shoved a slice of bacon into my mouth and brought the plate to the table. "So how was it, going back to the art store again after all this time away?"

I regretted the question as soon as I saw Jane blush.

"It was perfect, Carson," Bill said. "Thank you."

I'd like to think I had nothing to do with the art store or anything else they might have done last night. But if I asked why he just thanked me, I was afraid I'd get more information about them than I really wanted to know.

"Cool."

As soon as I started eating, they both stood and brought their dishes to the sink.

"We're going to go get ready. Flight leaves at noon, right?"

I nodded.

"Then we'll need to leave pretty soon or you won't get through security in time."

I glanced at the clock on the microwave.

Not sure how long it took other people to take off their belt and shoes, but I didn't need two hours. In fact, I could get Lane naked and ready for a strip search in less than a minute. But I didn't argue—as much as I liked this place and these people, I couldn't wait to get home.

"Thanks again, Carson," Jane said as they left.

"You're welcome?"

I couldn't hear individual words, but I recognized Lane's voice coming from the hallway. Since she was already smiling when she saw me, I figured she'd spoken to her parents while I was still asleep.

"I don't know what you said to my father yesterday, but it worked." She scooted a chair closer to mine and sat down. "Growing up, I never saw them unhappy, so I assumed they were happy. But it's pretty obvious now, isn't it? So, whatever it was, thank you."

I shrugged as she leaned in and kissed me. "I have a lot of bad karma to make up for."

When she pulled away a second later, I put my hand at the nape of her neck to stop her from getting too far. "I saved the day, remember? So I hope you weren't expecting me to be content with our lips touching."

"Fine." Her smile negated the eye roll she gave me. "But only because you saved the day."

I'm not sure how long we kissed. All I know is that I didn't give a shit if Jane or Bill or all the high school band kids came in —I wasn't going to let Lane go.

Until I heard the clink of dishes and remembered my breakfast.

"Get away from me, woman." I jokingly shoved her away and grabbed my fork. "I need to eat this before it gets cold."

"You're not doing anything at the end of May, are you?" She stole a piece of my toast and took a bite. Brave woman.

"Well, I have some showers planned... with soap. Probably some drinking. Definitely some eating and making love to you... and some eating *while* making love to you. Why?"

"Hillary and Eric just set a date for their wedding."

"Oh, goody." Yeah, that response didn't even sound a little bit excited.

"I know what you mean." She slumped back into her chair, taking the coffee cup out of my hand and gulping down a third of it. "Honestly, I'm so sick of everything to do with marriage— the beginnings of them and the fear of them ending. Why does everything have to be so dramatic?"

I took the cup back before she finished it. "Chicks dig drama, especially wedding drama."

"Not me. I don't want any of that. All I want is you and me, a couple friends, and maybe some music."

It was the first time she'd ever actually said what she wanted, other than during the makeup sex. And I'd learned not to believe anything anyone said during sex—her or me. But it did give me an idea.

Before we left for the airport, I pulled her mom into the guest room. "Jane, could I talk to you about something?"

"I think you've earned the right to talk to me about anything, Carson." She waited for me to speak. Then she gave up because it was taking me too damn long to figure out how to start. "Is it about your mother?"

"Definitely not. I promised Lane I wouldn't curse in front of you, so that makes talking about Renee impossible. Plus, I like you too much to subject you to anything I could say about her. I was just... um... wondering if you might be able to make it up to San Francisco the week after next. You and Bill. I'd be happy to get you tickets."

"We'd love to. But why so soon?"

"The reveal of the lobby installation Lane was contracted to do is in ten days. If you stayed the whole weekend, we could show you some of the city."

"We'd love to, Carson." She put her hand on my arm. "Thank you for inviting us."

"Lane would want you to be there. And... I'd like you to be there too." I'd spent my life hating the idea of mothers, but not anymore. First of all, I couldn't wait to help make Lane be one. Aside from the fun of the initial set-up, I wanted to know the little person who grew inside her, who'd have a childhood so different from mine. Who'd have an awesome mom, one fantastic grandma, and supervised visits with the other.

He'd—yes, still hoping for a boy, at least until I could handle a girl—have a good life. Because no matter how badly I screwed up, he'd still have a good male role model in Uncle Hayden. And his Aunt Andi could teach him what every kid should know, like how to hide porn on his computer when he hit puberty.

"I'd also like to surprise her with something," I said, running a hand through my hair, "but I'm still not exactly sure the best way..."

"To ask her?" Jane said smiling. How did she know?

"Yeah," I grumbled. "I wanted to give her the whole fairytale happy ending, but I'm not a fairytale kind of guy."

"What brought you two together, Carson?"

"Um..." A bad pickup line? The best first kiss ever? My self-sacrificing offer to fuck her without any strings attached? "I was kind of a jerk actually. But for some reason, she kept me around."

"Laney has never needed anyone to save her. She fell in love with you because she knew you were a good man. The man she needed—warts and all."

"Whoa, now." I put up both hands in submission, one hand in front of my mouth to hide my smile. "I don't know what she told you, but I've never had—

"Oh." I felt the truth hit me, what I'd been missing this whole time. Lane didn't need an extravagant, YouTube-worthy proposal. She could've gotten that from anyone. The reason she was with me was because I wasn't like all the other guys she'd dated. I never pretended to be a prince or a hero. I wasn't anything until I met her.

I looked around the room until I saw the book I'd been reading myself to sleep with. "Can I borrow this?"

As confused as she looked, Jane didn't hesitate. "Of course."

I grabbed it and flopped onto the foot of the bed, flipping through pages until I found it.

Jane sat next to me and read over my shoulder. "*The Frog Prince?*"

"Yep," I whispered.

The Frog Prince.
Our story.

35

CARSON

IT HAD BEEN nine days since we'd said goodbye to Lane's parents in San Diego. Nine days of Lane obsessing over every splinter of wood, every brush of urethane. Nine days of falling asleep before she'd come to bed and waking up after she'd already left.

Nine miserable days of seeing her so stressed out the only way I could get her to stop pacing was to pin her to the bed with my body.

Okay, that was a good afternoon.

But the rest were hell.

Her parents would be flying in later tonight. Maybe I'd get to play tour guide for the full day tomorrow so Lane could get in a little more panicking before her event started.

Obviously, this would be the best time to pile another stressor on top of everything else. And get it done in the twenty minutes between when Lane took an Uber from the building downtown to her shop, grabbed some emergency wax and rags and wood stuff, and came back here in the Uber.

I would've offered to go for her so she could stay here and micromanage the set-up of her tables and benches. But I had a stupid plan to execute. Plus Lane knew I would've grabbed the wrong stuff no matter how good her instructions were.

As soon as the door closed behind her, I grabbed my bag, ducked and weaved through her lily pad tables, and headed straight for the infinity fountain at the far end of the lobby.

A stone ledge defined the perimeter of the fountain with a five-inch wide moat running next to it all the way around. The water looked like it was topped with a huge sheet of glass right up to the very edge. From there, a tiny amount spilled over, forming a continuous waterfall that rained down into the moat and was pumped back up into the fountain—the *infinity* part of the infinity fountain.

I took the four-inch golden ball out of the hidden pocket in my bag and unwrapped it. It had to be rushed and custom made because, shockingly, not many people needed a watertight ball covered in sealed gold leaf that could also hold an engagement ring inside it. Well, not many people who hired the only guy I'd found in the city who could do it. I'm sure there was a big demand for them on the East Coast though.

Problem I should have anticipated number one: I didn't know how deep the water was. To get to it, I had to step up about a foot, and the ledge came up to around my knees. So the fountain could be knee deep, knee-plus-step deep, or *abyss*-deep for all I knew.

Problem number two: The guy had made the ball heavy enough to stay on the bottom of the fountain. So if I chucked it into the water, it might plummet to the bottom, crack open like an egg, and Lane's fancy ring would end up being nothing more than a very valuable shiny thing she could make a wish on. Until someone stole it.

With only about fifteen more minutes to get this done, I walked around the fountain, looking for a pole or floaties or—

"Net!" Perfect. A pool net with an extendable metal pole was leaning up against a tall supply closet decorated to look like vegetation, at the least-accessible end of the fountain.

I took it back to where I'd left my stuff, carefully set the ball into the net, and slowly lowered it into the water. I turned it over and shook the ball out about ten feet away from the ledge, where Lane would be able to see it when I casually brought her over here after the party.

Then I put the net back right where I'd found it and spent the next few minutes staring into the water, hoping this plan was "us" enough.

When Lane got back from her errand, I was hyperventilating in a corner. Luckily she was too preoccupied and tired to really notice.

Deep breaths. I could do this. Probably. Oh shit, what had I done? A golden fucking ball like in *The Frog Prince*? That was my great idea? It was worse than the last idea I thought was the worst ever. What I needed to do now was come up with a good idea to get *out* of this.

Okay. I'd wait until she was asleep tonight, then sneak back here and tell the security guard it was an emergency and I had to get inside the building.

What was the emergency? *Well, sir, I accidentally left my golden ball in the infinity fountain and needed to get it. Yep, in the middle of the night.*

Uh... no.

Okay, start over. I could get Hayden to distract her by—

"Are you fucking kidding me?" Lane said, looking down into the water. *Oh, crap.*

"Hey, babe!" I called back, pointing toward the other side of the lobby. "I think someone needs you to do something." Not a lie—I needed her to get the hell away from where she was before she saw my ball.

"Be there in a second. But first, I need your help, Carson. Some asshole tossed something in the fountain."

Not *some* asshole. Me. I was the asshole.

Yeah, it would be a total fail to let someone else fish the golden ball out, but you can't blame a guy for dreaming. I'd hoped *Lane* would have gotten it out herself, opened it, had a chance to weigh her options, and then come find me when she had an answer. Preferably a "Yes" answer.

"I can't tell what it is, but it shouldn't be in there." She leaned over the edge of the water, and I had a sudden flashback to the time she'd fallen into my bathtub, *our* bathtub now. "Can you believe people?"

I grabbed her arm and pulled her back a step. Ready to save another day, I went behind the fountain to grab the net. I knew exactly where I'd left it. *Aaand* fuck. It wasn't there.

"Maybe someone had a wish he needed to come true, babe."

I quickly searched through the supply closet, then around the entire fountain. Gone.

"In the middle of the lobby?" she grumbled. "What were they wishing for? A longer lunch?"

I'd only put it down fifteen minutes ago and hadn't seen anyone in this area who might've had an emergency requiring a pool net. So where the hell was it?

"Well," I called out, "maybe he was wishing the person he wanted to spend the rest of his life with would feel the same."

"Doubt it," she said. "Oh well. I'll ask the janitor to grab it tonight after we leave."

"I don't think that's a good idea." For a lot of reasons, including that I didn't want to marry a janitor. Without a more logical or dry solution, I kicked off my shoes and rolled up my jeans.

"What are you—?"

"Actually"—I climbed onto the ledge and tried to keep the grimace off my face as freezing cold water poured over my feet —"I bet that's exactly what he was thinking. He'd probably hoped she wouldn't see it until he had a pool net, but hey, can't have everything, right?"

"What are you talking about?"

"Nothing," I mumbled, slowly dipping one foot in and searching for the bottom with my toes. Not even close. So I sucked it up and started lowering myself into the water.

"Want to make a wish?" *My* only wish was that this water wasn't deep enough to reach my balls.

Another few inches and my wish wouldn't have come true.

"Carson, wait. You're getting soaked. Let's just ask someone from the building to grab it later."

"Nope. No, that's not a good idea." I waded through the water, clenching my teeth harder every time a new area of skin got wet. When the ball was just in front of my feet, I took a deep breath and steeled myself to reach for it.

"I'm exhausted, and you think now is a good time to go swimming? Can we please go home?"

"Just a sec, babe." I may have squealed as the chill soaked through my sleeve, but I got hold of the damn ball and yanked it out of the water.

"Is that—? What is that?" Her voice was tinged with suspicion, or maybe it was disbelief that her boyfriend had turned out to be such a wimp about frigid water. I didn't want to know.

As much as I wished I could run for the side and vault out of this arctic runoff, I walked back to her slowly, terrified of what I had to do next.

I kept the ball behind my back and ignored all the stares of the workmen who should've been minding their own business but obviously didn't want to miss the most humbling moment of my life.

"I finally read the original story of *The Frog Prince*," I said when I was a few feet away from her. "Turns out, I'd remembered it completely wrong. Do you know how the story goes?"

She inhaled deeply and then shook her head. "Tell me."

I couldn't feel the cold of the water anymore, had stopped caring that I was soaking wet or that people might be watching us.

Only one thing mattered now. Our story.

"Once upon a time, a beautiful princess accidentally dropped her golden ball into a pond." I slowly brought the ball in front of me and held it out to her. "Luckily, a devilishly handsome frog came along and agreed to get it back for her."

Her eyes were watering, darting between me and the ball. "In exchange for a kiss."

"Oh, so you've heard it?" When I smiled, I realized I wasn't even nervous anymore. This was Lane. How could I ever be afraid of Lane, other than a few days a month?

"I've never heard it quite like this," she said, biting her lip to keep it still.

"When we met, you told me you turned men into frogs. I never believed that, by the way. What I *did* believe was that you somehow turned this frog into a man." When I touched my chest, water flew off my sleeve and landed in my face.

Here's the big moment. Don't screw it up. "A man who wants to spend the rest of his life thanking you. And proving it was worth it."

I waited until I was just in front of her before I cracked open the orb. Carefully. Because I wasn't up to fishing a diamond out of the water.

When I separated the halves, Lane gasped and slapped her

hands over her mouth. Damn it, I was kind of hoping I could get an answer out of that thing.

"I'd get down on one knee," I said, "but this water would freeze both my balls, so…"

"Yes."

"Will you marry me?"

Her answer didn't register until she said it again. "Yes, Carson. Yes, I'll marry you." She took the ball from me, set it down on step, and took out her ring. "But only in exchange for a kiss."

"How about a lot of kisses?"

"If you insist."

One of the workmen tossed a towel at me. Since I was staring at the love of my life, I caught it with my shoulder and the side of my head.

"Gee, thanks." It wasn't much more than a rag, but I took it gratefully. I'd already screwed up more than I wanted to. With my luck, slipping on the water I tracked everywhere and landing on my ass would be what she remembered most.

Lane pulled me toward her by the collar. "Come here."

Actually, I take that back.

I don't think either of us would remember anything more than that kiss.

36

LANEY

I SPENT all day at the building downtown, frantically wiping down each of the bench/table combos I'd built. As if everyone would hate them if there were a single fingerprint on them. As if there wouldn't be thousands of new fingerprints on every single surface every single day after the lobby had officially been revealed and hundreds of people trudged through the area tomorrow.

After all, I made furniture. Beautiful, sleek-looking pieces of art, but still furniture. And furniture was meant to be used.

The people who brought their grubby hands through here tomorrow on their way to work or appointments would obviously want to touch them, trace the lines in each piece of wood I'd painstakingly chosen for its beauty, then carved, formed, sanded, and lacquered. Laptops, purses, and phones would be dumped on them carelessly by those who didn't see them the same way I did. Who didn't know how hard I'd worked or how proud I was of each piece.

At five o'clock, I had to let it go and get ready for the unveiling. First thing I did was carefully take my new engagement ring out of its necklace setting and slip it back onto my finger.

It was heavy and I was still getting used to wearing it, but man, did I love it. I knew it would only take a few days before I'd start to feel naked without it on my finger.

I raced home to shower and change into my gown. Not a dress, a gown. Less like a Cinderella-type puff and more like something on the red carpet at the Academy Awards.

It was white, form-fitting most of the way down, and made my boobs look great. The chiffon layers of the lower part bounced with every step I took and made me feel beautiful from the second I tried it on at Hillary's house. She'd bought it as an engagement gift to herself a week ago. But, when I went by her and Eric's place this morning and told her my plan for tonight, she screamed, sprinted in and back out of their bedroom, and shoved a garment bag into my arms.

Inside was the most perfect thing I'd ever seen.

I slipped into it, adjusted my breasts, then put my robe on top, carefully tucking up the chiffon pieces that hung out. Not only would the extra layer of coverage keep me from getting makeup on it, I also didn't want Carson to see it until we were at the event.

I wore my hair up in a twist and put my makeup on with more care than I'd ever used, following one of the countless YouTube tutorials I'd nervously watched every chance I could all day.

Huh. Smudging eyeliner was not the same as smearing it. Damn it, I should've practiced earlier. Or watched more what-*not*-to-do tutorials.

I cursed and started over, wondering why I'd spent so damn much money on fancy new makeup when it would've been so much smarter to buy fancy new hands that knew how to use the shit.

Carson was probably in shock that I was putting so much effort in, but he didn't say anything. All he had to do to look fantastic was put on a suit and run a hand through his hair, the bastard. He watched me silently with a small smile on his lips as I frantically, but gently, wiped the mess off my face. If I rubbed any harder, I would've had to color-correct for the redness, and I had no idea how to do that.

"Stop staring!"

"Stop worrying, babe." He pushed off the doorjamb he'd been leaning on and gave me a hug. "Believe me, from what I can see of that dress, no one's going to be able to take their eyes off your rack long enough to see your face."

"Cute, but not helpful." I pulled the neck of the robe higher and retied the belt. Then I shoved him out of my way so I could get back to work. "Go away."

He laughed. "Lane, you're gorgeous without all that crap. Just take a deep breath."

I tried. In for two, out for two.

"That was unbelievably hot." His eyes rested firmly on my terrycloth-covered chest. "Do it again. Please."

"You're such a dick." A dick who somehow always knew how to make me smile.

"Yeah well"—He pointed at his chest—"*this* dick"—and then at his crotch—"and *this* dick will both be leaving in ten minutes. If you're not ready, you'll have to walk there, alone. At night. Looking like that. So I suggest you hurry."

I knew he'd never leave without me, but having a deadline helped me get over myself and focus.

Despite my best efforts and incredible will, sadly I didn't magically turn into a supermodel. But I looked good, I *felt* good, and asking for more would just be greedy.

"One minute till departure," he yelled from the living room.

I grabbed my shoes and hopped into them as I moved. Makeup? Check. Hair done-ish? Check. Dress and shoes? Check. Bag?

"Damn it, where'd I put my—?"

He stood in the open doorway, my purse hanging over his shoulder.

"Fuck, you're gorgeous, babe. But more importantly, how do *I* look?"

Until now, I'd thought the reveal of my first commissioned art installation was what made this night the most important of my life. I'd fought all my doubts, along with the doubts of everyone I'd ever met, that I could make it as an artist.

Actually, that wasn't true. Carson had never doubted me. Not once.

"Are robes part of a new trend I don't know or care about?"

"Oops." I looked down at myself. "Right. I'll be one more second." I grabbed my coat and went back into the bedroom so he couldn't see me. I dumped the robe, ran my hands over the dress, then covered its gorgeousness back up with a coat that was way too long and too heavy for the weather.

When I came out, he was staring at his watch.

"Geez, Carson! Come on already! We need to go."

Smiling, he held the door for me, whispering, "You got this, babe," as I went past him.

"Thanks for putting up with me." And just like that, all the stress and anxiety I'd had about the evening was completely gone.

And just like that, it all came flooding back as soon as we pulled up to the building. There were already people standing around, dressed up and chatting on the steps leading up to the front doors.

Carson took care of the valet and came around the car to get me. I hadn't even opened the door.

"You coming?" he asked after opening it. He waited for my reply—one that didn't come—and then pulled me out of the car.

"I think it's time for a reality check, babe. As amazing as you are and as your art is, none of these people are here for that. They came for the free booze, fancy snacks, and to show off their wardrobes. Okay?" With one arm around my waist and his other hand squeezed in between both of mine, he walked/pushed me up the steps and into the building.

"I swear to you, Lane, in an hour, they won't even remember what your face looks like. All they'll remember is how sexy you are, how great you are with wood, and the bad pun they could make putting those two things together. Everything else they'll black out. The best part is, we don't care. Because the only thing we want them to remember is your name every time they pass through this lobby."

"You're right." Or he would've been right in any other circumstance. But tonight I'd be doing a lot more than blushing, shaking hands, and thanking people.

He gasped when he helped me out of my coat and got the full view of my gown. "Holy shit, babe. You're fucking beautiful. I take back everything I said before—they're *all* going to remember what you look like. I know *I* don't plan on ever forgetting how gorgeous you look tonight."

"Always so charming," I teased, but inside I was doing a little celebratory dance. He loved the dress as much as I did.

37

LANEY

THEY'RE HERE to see the lobby, not to see me. They're here to see the lobby, not to see me.

This thought came back to me every few minutes throughout the reception. When people came up to congratulate me for creating something so beautiful, so complex and meaningful, all I could focus on was the ring on my finger and what was going to happen after John's dedication speech.

Carson was intent on making sure I met everyone who had anything to do with the art world, architecture, and design. So I couldn't spend nearly enough time with the people I actually *wanted* to talk to—Hillary and Eric, my mom and dad, Hayden and Andi, even Renee and Anna.

Right after a woman I'd never seen before and I were done air-kissing and I'd finished thinking, *"Who the hell decided air-kissing should be a thing? Why can't we just say hello and be done with it?"* she grabbed my hand.

Her eyes widened when she spotted the ring, not that it was very hard to spot, of course. "Oh, honey, congratulations!" Was she congratulating me for my engagement or for getting a great ring? "It's gorgeous!"

Guess I'd been right to wonder. Should I thank her? I had nothing to do with picking it out, other than landing a guy with great taste who knew me incredibly well.

Perfect. "Thank you so much." For recognizing my incredible taste in *the* man I *planned* to marry.

I couldn't blame her. My ring was a gorgeous piece of jewelry and an even more gorgeous symbol of how amazing our future would be.

Carson stood next to me the whole night, guiding me around and telling me when to stop being afraid and staring at the floor, so I wouldn't seem rude to the guests at the party.

He was right and wrong. I didn't want to be rude to anyone, but that's not why I was acting weird. Most of them had no idea what the most important part of tonight was. Not even Carson.

"Laney!" I glanced up to see John, the owner of the building and the one who'd hired me to design and build the installation. "People can't stop telling me how beautiful your work is. And I can't stop thinking how beautiful *you* are. So congratulations. I'm not sure if anything could make this night more special."

When John winked at me, Carson pulled me a little closer to him, completely misinterpreting John's intent. I wasn't worried —he'd find out soon enough.

Then I looked to the woman on John's arm. "Geez, Anna. You know everybody, don't you?"

"There are probably a few people I've never met." Anna's eyes twinkled. But tonight, the twinkle wasn't because she was messing with me or trying to ruin my evening. Tonight it was because I'd let her in on my secret, too.

I'd only shared my plan with the people who had to know: John, to get his permission; my dad, because he'd spent most of today at the courthouse getting a special one-day officiant's permit; and my mom because I couldn't *not* tell her. Obviously, Hillary and Eric knew, and I'd called Hayden this afternoon to ask if he'd bring his side of the family. Right after hanging up with him, I'd called Anna, figuring a private invitation was the only way to get her to come. I almost lost it completely when I heard how excited she was to have been included.

Actually, that was a lot of people. Oh shit. This was real.

"You ready for this, Laney?" she asked quietly.

Ready? Probably not. But I couldn't wait, and I knew it was the right thing to do. "One hundred and fifty percent."

Carson tensed when his stepsister leaned in closer to me, assuming she was going to pull a ninja move in five-inch heels, I guess. He grunted a warning when she wrapped her arms around me to give me a quick hug. Right before she pulled away from me, Anna quietly and politely told him to shut the hell up.

Family.

"Okay then. Let's do this." John and Anna walked up to a small podium next to the infinity fountain where the planning committee was already standing, smiling at me knowingly. Dang it, had John told everyone? Anna? My stupidly proud and happy parents?

How many people did it take to keep a secret? Oh well, in a few minutes, it wouldn't matter.

"Ladies and gentlemen, can I have your attention please?" John said into a microphone. Once the crowd had quieted, he continued. "Because of the tireless work of many, many individuals, I stand before you tonight to celebrate the unveiling of our new lobby. It's gorgeous, isn't it?" He waited for the applause to die down. "This lobby is an homage to our beautiful city and its amazingly talented and complex community. We're here to celebrate art and, in a recent addition to tonight's festivities, we're also here to celebrate love."

"Please tell me he's not about to confess his undying love for you," Carson whispered. "Because I got there first."

I shushed him, not wanting to miss a second of this moment.

He gasped. "Oh fuck, what if he's going to propose to Anna? I gotta warn him! Or hurt him, maybe."

I put my hand on his arm and gave him a squeeze. "John's gay, Carson."

"You say that as if it would stop her from manipulating him into marriage."

"So without further ado..." John looked at me. "Laney, want to come up here and get this thing started?"

I nodded, glanced at Carson, and took his hand.

"Go let everybody tell you how great you are, babe," Carson said right before I started pulling him along with me. "Okay. I was going to heckle you from back here, but sure, I'll come if you want me to."

"You're not the only one who can plan a surprise," I said quietly.

"What's going on, Lane?" He came with me because he trusted me, but his steps were wary and his eyes confused. He must have noticed my father getting settled next to the podium with Hayden on one side and Hillary on the other.

"Look carefully at the benches and tables surrounding you, everyone," John said. "The first time I saw Laney's art, I thought it was beautiful, because... well, because I'm not blind." Small chuckle from the audience. "But until she brought her sketches to me and we started talking, I didn't know how much passion she had, how much of who she *is* she put into her work, along with her incredible skill.

"And, before we go any further, I should tell you that Carson Bennett proposed to Laney in this very water yesterday."

Carson groaned as the crowd *awwed* and applauded.

"Are your pants dry yet, Carson?"

"Wow. I really wish he hadn't said it like that." Carson pulled me forward a few steps to get away from whoever had tried to pat him on the back. "Can't wait to see the headline on tomorrow's gossip page."

"Anyway," John said. "When I heard about the proposal, I remembered an early conversation Laney and I had. She told me her design would represent the steps we all have to take to reach our goals."

I stood there nervously with Carson, listening to John explain the for-public-consumption meaning I'd told him after realizing I wanted to keep the real one between me, Carson, and the people who loved us. Now I wished I'd given John an even simpler version because it was taking him *forever* to explain it to the crowd. I saw a few guests lose interest and go to the bar or step outside. Fine with me—I didn't want anyone to stay for what happened next if they didn't want to.

"And before we can move to the next lily pad," John said, pointing to the tables one-by-one, "we have to find balance on each so we don't fall into the water—i.e., make a catastrophic mistake—on our way to getting where we want to be. Each step..."

"Are you sure he isn't in love with you?" Carson whispered. "If I'd known how long-winded he'd be, I would've gotten another drink."

"Shut up." It came out a little harsher than I'd wanted it to. I added, "And listen to how great people think I am," so he wouldn't notice how my nerves were gaining control over me with every passing second.

"...even more blessed because..."

"It's nothing I don't already know, babe. In fact, I think he's playing your greatness down so Anna won't slug him out of jealou—"

"...wanted to marry him in front of all of us. Right now."

"Wait. What did he just say?" Carson asked loudly. But it was nothing in comparison to the gasps and applause from the crowd.

I didn't look, but I imagined Carson's eyes ballooning out like a cartoon character's. Okay, I had to peek to know for sure.

No cartoon eyes, but he was turning in every direction, probably looking to see who John might have been talking about. But everyone was staring at us.

"You never listen, do you?" I asked, my eyes filling up with water while I waited for it to sink in.

38

LANEY

"HE WASN'T—?" Carson took one more look at all the eyes fixed on us, looked down at me, and then nodded his head. "He was. He was talking about us." His eyes changed as he started to put things together. "That amazing dress. Why your folks were so busy today. Anna being nice. You set me up."

I shrugged. "I got impatient."

"In twenty-four hours?"

"Are you mad?"

"That I didn't think of it? Nah, I love your surprises." With the corners of his mouth slowly lifting into a grin, he took my face in his hands and leaned in close, cutting everything else off. "You're sure want to do this? Because there's no backsies."

"No backsies," I repeated.

He took a deep breath. "Well, then I guess we're—"

Hayden grabbed him from behind and dragged him toward the podium. "Shut up and marry the woman, little brother. Before she really gets to know you."

My dad appeared at my side, holding out his elbow for me to take it. He had the best timing ever, because I thought I was about to faint.

My mom was already sobbing and hiding her face behind a tissue. I wasn't sure if Hillary's tears were from happiness or because she was biting her lower lip so hard in a vain attempt to hold them back. I assumed Eric was somewhere in the crowd taking pictures because that's just what he did.

When I saw a hand waving, it took me a minute to see through my overwhelming nervousness and realize the hand belonged to Andi. Sara, Emilia and Rob stood next to her smiling.

Dear God, why was everyone smiling so much? All those exposed teeth made me feel like I was surrounded by a pack of growling wolves.

I faltered, nervous as hell to stand up in front of all these people and do this. Sure, it had been my idea, but maybe it was a bad one. Maybe I could switch directions, grab Carson on the fly, and run for an emergency exit. Seriously, if this wasn't an emergency, nothing was.

Carson caught my eye and smiled. How could he be so calm? After telling me how long he'd been freaking out about proposing?

He mouthed something I think was, "Get your ass up here so I can marry you already, woman." I'd never been happier to have him take control. Stop me from making a mistake, from doing something I'd regret. From letting fear keep me away from something so good, I hadn't even had the guts to dream of it.

After a deep breath, I nodded. "Yes, sir." I smiled at the surprised look on his face, hoping he knew that comment was as close to me obeying him as he'd ever get. Then I relaxed my shoulders and walked up to the front with my dad holding about half my body weight so I wouldn't fall over.

My dad, ever the traditionalist, even in such an untraditional setting, "gave me away" by putting my hands into Carson's.

Carson's face flashed white when Dad whispered, "You hurt

her, and I'm going to take you on a one-way deep sea fishing trip. Understand, son?"

"I hate fishing, Bill, so we're good."

While my dad introduced himself to the crowd and told them an embarrassing story from my sophomore year of high school, Carson and I just looked at each other, holding hands, me breaking into a goofy, lovesick grin occasionally.

"My daughter never did like church much and, if I wasn't so sure these two people were meant to be together, I might've questioned Laney's plan. But they understand each other like no one else I know. They know how to make each other happy. And, just a guess here, but I think this is making them happy, don't you?"

The crowd laughed.

I was more than happy. There were no goody bags, big cake, or months of planning, no time for last minute jitters or panic— other than what I was feeling right now—but everyone important to us was there.

My dad pointed the microphone toward me. "Would you two like to say anything to each other before we get to the legal stuff?"

"Not fair, Lane," Carson said quietly. "You had time to plan out what you were going to say."

Yeah, tons of time, when I wasn't doing three other things today.

"Tell me the truth, Carson. In your entire life, have you ever planned out anything you've ever said?"

He thought about it for a second. "I see your point. But you go first, so I know what I'm up against."

I would've loved to kiss the smirk off his face, but we had to save the kissing until the end.

"When I was—" Hearing my own voice through the speakers, a second after I said something, threw me off. I scooted closer to Carson to see if that helped. I knew he didn't mind—he moved one of his hands to my waist as if that's where it was meant to be.

I agreed. "When I was a little girl"—thankfully, the reverb was gone—"and believed in fairytales, I dreamt of a huge wedding hall with high ceilings and a big chandelier. A hundred beautifully dressed people would be there to watch me marry my very own prince charming."

Everyone looked up to the lobby's giant glass chandelier. Everyone but Carson.

"But only after I'd grown up and stopped believing in fairytales did I actually find one. The real kind. The kind that will keep going long after a happy ending kiss.

"Now, standing here in front of a hundred people, all beautifully dressed, I get to marry my prince. Whether he wants to or not."

Carson was biting his lip, but his eyes were laughing.

I lowered my voice and spoke only to him. "I mean honestly, if it took you as long as you say it did just to work up the courage to *ask* me, you'd never have been ready to set a date. Hope you don't mind."

"Are you kidding? This is the craziest, best idea you've ever had." Staring at my mouth, the hand on my waist pulled me forward and he leaned toward me. Unfortunately, he caught himself before he got too close.

My dad flipped the microphone around and waited for Carson to start.

"Oh. Is it my turn now?" He swallowed, took a deep breath, and then looked into my eyes. When he spoke, it was only to me. "I've been thinking a lot about the day we met lately. Remember? When I saw you in our café and decided I really wanted to"—quick glance at my dad—"spend the afternoon with you."

I laughed at his PG-13 explanation of that day. I couldn't

imagine what would've happened if he'd told the truth—the only thing Carson had wanted to do that day was get laid.

"I had no idea what I was about to walk into," he said. "Getting to know you, getting to *love* you, are the best things that have ever happened to me. When *I* was a little girl"—

Laughing gave me a second to regroup, stop my lip from trembling and my eyes from tearing up.

—"I didn't know any fairytales. Well, I did, but I don't remember any of them having a happy ending. The only ones I can remember were pretty scary, confusing to a kid. Lots of big bad wolves, you know?"

I pressed my lips together to stop myself from whimpering, but I couldn't control the tears. In a room full of people, only a few of us understood what he was really talking about. Hayden and Renee because they'd been there. Anna because she'd gone through a similar reality with *her* father.

"When I grew up, I think I still believed in them a little. That's what I figured my life would be—witches, and frogs, and no happy ending."

When he wiped away a tear I'd missed near my jaw, I leaned into his hand and rested my cheek there.

"And then you came along and, as hard as I tried to tell myself I didn't care about you, I felt myself falling for you every minute of every day that we spent together. And I started to believe that maybe, because of you, there might be a happy ending or two in my future."

When he smirked at the double entendre, I held my breath, flicking my head toward my dad to remind Carson it wasn't just him and me standing here. I knew he'd gotten my hint when his smile disappeared.

"Anyway," he said, readjusting himself. "I want to be the man you deserve, Lane. But being that great ain't easy for anyone, and it's next to impossible for *me*. So it may take me sixty or seventy years to do it, but if you stick around, I promise I'll never stop trying."

I nodded. "I think I can do sixty or seventy years."

"Great," he said, taking a deep breath and turning to my dad. "Do I get to kiss her now?"

"Not quite yet." My dad's eyes were red, but his voice was controlled when he asked Hayden and Hillary to bring us the rings.

I guess Carson and I said what we were supposed to because the next thing I really remember is each of us wearing a new ring and Carson's hand cupping the nape of my neck and pulling me toward him.

His lips were so warm and soft as they met mine. We'd kissed ten thousand times, and it never got old or expected. I never wanted to stop. I never got distracted. All I wanted was more.

He pulled me in tighter, opening his mouth enough to taste me, to let me taste him. Every time we kissed felt like the very first time, a chance to discover each other, to be closer, to connect.

I heard myself moan when it was too late to stop it from coming out. Carson's lips pulled away from mine when he smiled.

But the worst was when I heard my dad say, "There's probably a better place for you two to finish that up."

I heard some clapping, yelling, and laughing. I was inundated with hugs from family, friends, and complete strangers as they congratulated me. But the only thing I could focus on was Carson's beaming smile.

Once the only ones left around us were our loved ones, Carson turned to Clare. "Can you plan a party for us? Whatever you want to do. Open bar, big cake, and a bouquet for Lane to throw. And make sure you invite everyone here and everyone from the Foundation—staff *and* families."

"Clare, I'd love to help you," Anna said. "Whatever you need."

"Okay." Still smiling, Carson leaned toward his sister and kissed her on the cheek. "No poison apples though, right?"

"I can't make any promises."

"I'll be keeping an eye on you, sis. But not until I get back from my honeymoon." Carson swept me up in his arms and headed for the exit. "So where are you taking me? I'm thinking clothing optional." I didn't even have time to roll my eyes, before he continued, "Someplace we won't see another person for weeks, months maybe."

I put my arms around his neck. "And no jellyfish."

"Definitely no jellyfish." He spun me around and yelled. "Thanks, everybody. For guiding me to this moment *and* this woman."

I waved goodbye to the people I loved and was carried away by the man I'd be with forever.

My frog.

My prince.

My husband.

Once Upon a Time...

...THERE WAS *a man who finally convinced the most beautiful woman in the world that they would live happily ever after. For "happily ever after" didn't mean they'd never be unhappy, or irritable, or overwhelmed. Nor did it mean they would always know what the other was thinking before any words were spoken, or that they would never make a mistake.*

For this couple, as with all others who are destined to be, "happily ever after" means they will never give up... on themselves or on each other.

The End

~

Flip the next few pages to read the first chapter of Immaterial Defense (Once and Forever #4)

Thank you so much for reading Deeper Water.

If you enjoyed the book, *please* consider leaving a review. Reviews can make or break the success of a book, so they're greatly appreciated.

Want more?

Sign up for my newsletter to get exclusive extras and be notified when future books in this series are available. Visit my website to get started!

www.LaurenStewartAuthor.com

Immaterial Defense
(Once and Forever #4)

∾

Two strangers meet in a karaoke bar.

She's all alone in the darkness.
He's lighting up the stage.

It's going to take a whole lot longer than one night to get all they
need from each other.

∾

Book #4 is a party-girl/rockstar twist on The Emperor's New
Clothes. Keep turning pages to read the first chapter.
But first, this is how Sara's fairytale begins...

*Once upon a time there was a woman whose life had been blessed
from the moment of her birth. She wore beautiful gowns, and went to
fancy balls, and danced with handsome princes, and hated every
second of it. For, though none but the woman knew it, these things
were not real but imagined. And the reason the woman understood
this was because she wasn't real either, having been unmade in a
single moment in time...by an enemy she hadn't foreseen...in a way
that left her body wounded and her soul scarred.*

 *So the woman began a new life, apart from all others, even while
surrounded by admirers, for she knew they were admiring someone
who wasn't real, whose truth couldn't be seen by their eyes. Though*

outwardly people still believed her to be beautiful and blessed, inwardly she knew it wasn't true. And though her appearance and wealth continued to bring compliments and accolades, she saw what none other could—that for the rest of her nonexistence, she would be invisible to all...

Chapter 1

- Sara -

Oh crap. That was bad. Not like bad-sex bad. In fact, what we just did was *nothing* like bad sex. Which made it bad in the *too-good-sex* way. And everyone knows that too-good sex with a guy you barely know is bad. Because if the sex is that good the first time, you want to see what it would be like the second time...and the twentieth. And then you get attached, even if he turns out to be a horrible dickhead in every other way.

All because he gave you multiple orgasms.

I know this not from personal experience, but because at some unfortunate in our biological development, women have decided that if a man cares enough to figure out what you need to get off, he cares about the person attached to the vagina.

Therefore, this man was dangerous in an emotional way, which made it way worse because physical injuries heal a lot quicker than emotional ones do.

So as soon as I'd caught my breath, I slid out of his bed and looked for my clothes.

"What are you doing?" he asked, sitting up.

"I'm going home. It's past my bedtime."

Damn, he was gorgeous. His spiky light brown hair looked even better than it had before the last few hours of full-body wrestling we'd just done. A small dimple dented each of his cheeks, even though he wasn't smiling anymore. A body Greek sculptors could only fantasize about. I could feel a purr of longing starting in my stomach. Okay, fine, it may have started a little lower than my stomach.

I wanted to go over and kiss him one more time, but that would risk him pulling me back in for another round. I slipped on my undies and then my pants.

"Huh. Okay. So what'd you use me for?"

"I—" I didn't look up. And I didn't answer his question.

Then he was in front of me, his hands on my waist. "Is this the first time you've done it?"

I laughed. "Wow. Was I that bad?"

"The sex? No, the sex was fantastic. Phenomenal. But I meant, is this the first time you've buttoned up your pants?"

"I don't get it."

"Look at me." He repeated it when I hesitated, then smiled when I raised my chin and made eye contact. "Well, there has to be a reason you would be so focused on your jeans that you couldn't even bother to look at me. So buttoning your pants... It's pretty easy once you get the hang of it. I'll show you." He brushed my hands out of the way and buttoned my jeans, holding my eyes and feeling his way through the process. "See? Don't worry. You'll get it eventually. And then you won't even have to look." He pulled me towards him. "Now kiss me."

I shook my head and ran my lip through my teeth. "I probably have terrible morning breath."

"This is a continuation of last night. You have to sleep to have morning breath. So kiss me already."

I did, lightly until his lips demanded more. My arms stayed to my sides, stuck there immobile, the only thing with any control whatsoever it seemed, because the rest of my body responded to his every touch. His tongue slipped inside my mouth and his arms wrapped tightly around me, lifting me up onto my tip toes.

He pulled away slightly and lowered me to the ground. "You're right. You have terrible morning breath." His smile was wicked. "That was such a horrible experience, I'd like to do it again. Right now."

"I need to go."

He released me, sighing. "If I asked you for your number so we could see each other again, would you give me a fake one?"

I shook my head. "I'd just say no."

"Fuck, that's harsh," he said, running his hand through his hair. "A guy could take that personally, you know."

"You shouldn't. You were great, and you seem like a nice guy. But I never give my number out."

"So either you're already involved or you have serious issues. Which is it?"

"I'm not already involved with anyone."

He grimaced and then went to his dresser. "If you ever want to be, give me a call." He took a business card out of his wallet, wrote something down on it, and handed it to me. "It's not my card, but I wrote down my number. Call me."

"Me and my issues?"

"We all have issues, Sara. And we all have ways to cope."

"How do you cope?"

"Self-destructively. I'm really good at it. Last night, for example, I went to a bar looking for an amazing woman who would want nothing to do with me in the morning. All so that I can spend the next few days pounding my head against the wall wondering what happened and where I went wrong. Totally successful endeavor, by the way. In fact, it's probably better that you don't give me your number because I'm going to be busy telling myself what a fuck-up I am until...at least, Thursday or Friday."

I curled my fingers around his card instead of giving it back like I'd planned. "I don't do the relationship thing."

"Obviously." He held up his hands and motioned to himself. "'Cause, if you did, how could you possibly pass this mess up?"

"Maybe we could just..." I shrugged. Damn it. He was ten times as gorgeous as anyone I'd ever been with, had an incredible body he knew exactly how to use, and a sense of humor I could definitely get used to. Which made him complicated. And another hook-up would be dangerous, regardless of how much I'd like to.

"Okay, I think I finally got your hint," he said nodding. "Well, Sara. It was nice to meet you, it was great to fuck you, and I wish you, your issues, and your coping mechanisms long and happy lives."

"Same to you. I'm gonna...I mean, I could..."

"If you want to leave, then leave. If you want to stay, then stay. Shit, if you need a coin to toss, I'll give you one. But I'm feeling slightly insecure right now, so would appreciate it if you could make a decision without any more of the mixed signals."

He was right—my actions *defined* mixed signals, because that was all my mind could manage right now. What needed to happen was a decision. The same one I always made, in the past year, at least.

"Bye." I ran. I didn't close the doors behind me, as if my subconscious was hinting that I didn't want those doors to close. But it could go to hell. I knew what I wanted, and it wasn't him. It wasn't any of them. The only person I could count on was myself. I was the only one who could keep me safe. I was the only one I could trust.

When I got to the sidewalk, I took out the card he'd given me and smoothed it on my pant leg. Some guy who was a music executive of some kind. But on the other side, there was a name and a number—Declan. Declan. It was a nice name. Nice guy. A nice guy with a nice name that I would never be seeing again.

Besides, he was wrong—one-nighters weren't coping mechanisms. They were distractions, something to relieve the pressure and blow off steam. Two people getting what they want without the inevitable hurt that depending or trusting someone leads to.

Did some people think I had trust issues? Hell yes. But I saw myself as a realist. No one should trust anyone. That was a fact.

No one saw pain coming, or it wouldn't hurt so much when it happened. You wouldn't feel humiliated and spend weeks in shock, living in a blurred reality. That wouldn't happen if you were prepared, stayed vigilant, didn't look for things that weren't real. The only thing you can trust is that people are liars and do whatever the hell they want to do without concern for anyone else.

I hadn't been prepared once, and it had almost killed me. A mistake I'll never repeat. Ever.

Seriously, folks, this one both breaks my heart and cracks me up. Can't wait to share Sara and Declan's story with you.

Plus, stay tuned for my twists on The Little Mermaid, Rapunzel, Rumplestiltskin, Cinderella, Peter Pan, and the Princess and the Pea.

ALSO BY LAUREN STEWART

The Heights

Unseen, Vol 1

Job security isn't something Addison is all that concerned with. Death, however? Yeah, death is a major concern.

While a prophesied war brews in the Heights, Addison and Rhyse must decide which carries more risk—trusting someone who could destroy you or trusting someone who could *love* you?

Unearthed, Vol 2

What would you give up for freedom? Even if it wasn't yours?

Two people from opposite sides of a war will discover the price of freedom and what they're willing to pay for it. But in the Heights, nothing is ever fair. For something they both want, one of them will pay with their eternity.

Unwanted, Vol 3

~ coming soon ~

The werewolf pack doesn't want Noah almost as much as he doesn't want to be one of them. It doesn't get any easier when he realizes what he *does* want and where he truly belongs - next to the daughter of his most dangerous enemy.

~ This series is a mixture of urban fantasy and paranormal romance with multiple interlocking stories and characters and plot lines as well as different races of supernatural beings, each with their own cultures, hierarchy, and attributes. It's not a series about only two people, or three, or even four. This is a world in which everyone will have to pick a side. ~

The Hyde Trilogy

Hyde ~ Jekyll ~ Strange Case
The Complete Hyde Series Box Set

"...my favorite series of the year...

a perfect blend of what makes a book go down in history."

— Ohhh My Shelves

Dark and light, good and evil—mankind's universal struggle.

But what if you're not a man? Or can never allow yourself to be kind? What about on those nights when you're not quite human?

Two people bonded by a curse of heredity and the manipulation of an unknown entity. When the truth leaves them nothing to hold onto, they will be forced into a partnership neither expected...or wanted.

Because in life, who you trust is as important as who you *are*. And when you can't even trust yourself, sometimes the only person you can rely on is the last person on earth you should be falling for.

~ All three full-length novels are intended for adults because of very naughty language, biting sarcasm, and descriptive love scenes. They are not a retelling of the classic story. Not even close. ~

∾

Second Bite

A second chance...

A second lifetime...

Can Daniel overcome two lifetimes of guilt and be the man Olivia needs? Or will both of them lose everything?

Once and Forever

Darker Water #1

Some fairytales *begin* with a kiss...

Two people want the same thing--a commitment to nothing more than great sex in a bunch of different positions. Simple. Enjoyable. A win-win. Problem is, those two people have families and fears and pain that spill into every moment of their lives. And if either Carson or Laney can't free themselves from the past, they'll both be pulled under by it.

Virtually Impossible #2

Love *before* first sight...

Hayden and Andi need to wake up to understand how perfect they are...for each other. If they can't, any chance either of them have of finding a happily ever after will be virtually impossible.

Deeper Water #3

Carson and Laney's *After* Happily-Ever-After

Immaterial Defense #4

No one would believe her truth, so Sara almost starts believing her own lies. But after one incredible night with Declan, she realizes he can see past her beauty and into the pain she hides. And he won't give up on her until it's gone.

~ Once and Forever is a series of standalone romances inspired by the themes of classic tales and legends. Because while fairytales aren't real, love is. ~

No Experience Required

a Summer Rains mystery

After leaving the hippie commune she grew up on, Summer Rains set a modest goal for herself: earn enough money to live a normal life in the real world.

Maybe she was aiming too high.

~ This novel is a fun comedic-mystery, similar in tone to the books of Janet Evanovich, Meg Cabot, and Stephanie Bond. Also available as an audiobook. ~

≈

There will be more.

Much more. More in The Heights, Once and Forever, Summer Rains, a spin-off of the Hyde series, an as-of-now untitled YA paranormal series, and a billion more projects all impatiently waiting their turn. So stay in touch to find out what's next.

www.LaurenStewartAuthor.com

laurenstewartauthor@gmail.com

www.facebook.com/laurenstewartauthor

ww.twitter.com/readlaurens

Become a Stewartist! Join my Facebook reader's group to chat about books, life, and anything else we come up with.

Typically, this is where I give out advanced reader copies, swag, and lots of eBooks and signed paperbacks.

www.facebook.com/groups/laurenstewartauthor

ACKNOWLEDGMENTS

To my Stewartists, readers, bloggers, and writer buddies: Thank you for not giving up on me. It's an honor to call you friends. And no, I'm not going to stop calling you friends, no matter how many times you tell me to leave you alone.

To my talented and patient cover designer Amanda: You really should count yourself lucky to work with me. The amount of patience you've been forced to attain in order to deal with me is the only reason you'll ever get into heaven. ;)

AND ON THAT NOTE...

Dear reader:

Last year and most of 2016, I couldn't write. There were a lot of reasons for it - a car accident, a broken hand, physical therapy, anxiety, lots of different family health issues, moving, kids, the death of a parent.

It sucked. And not a day went by that I didn't feel guilty about it. Writing is freedom to me. It's exciting, and absorbing, and fun, and somehow makes time move five times faster. Since I didn't start doing it until 2010, I really wonder what kept me going all the years before that. Writing is a dream, a passion, and the thing I was meant to do.

But I couldn't do it.

I had all these incredible people asking me when my next book would be out and telling me to hurry the hell up.* I had some momentum in this crazy tough business, and my dream of writing full-time seemed completely doable.

Except I couldn't do it.

I hated that I was letting readers down. I hated that I was letting myself down. And the worse I felt, the longer I stayed away from my keyboard. And the fewer daydreams of banter or plot twists came to me.

Because I was afraid of disappointing someone, I held myself back from doing something that gives me a sense of self and makes me happy.

I'm not going to do that again. No one can, or should, live in fear of anything - real or imagined. I'm so grateful for everyone who's ever opened one of my books and, while I dearly hope you love every single one of them, I know you won't. And I have to be okay with that.

I started writing to express myself, to have fun, to get the crazy out of my head and onto the page. That's where I need to get back to. So I may disappear from social media occasionally or have a surprise release because I didn't want to stress out over all the prep of a big book launch.

I hope you'll be there and will continue to drop me notes, tell me what I *have* to read next, and nag me about my next release. Because I think you're amazing. And one thing I've always been great at is judging someone's character. Except for anyone I've dated and married. I'm really, really bad at picking those. :)

XOXOXO

- Lauren

*To everyone who encouraged me by emailing and sending messages to remind me what I should've been doing. It took a lot longer than any of us like, but it worked. So thank you.

ABOUT THE AUTHOR

Lauren Stewart lives in Northern California with one teenager, an almost-teenager, a cat, and a very big, very high-maintenance puppy. On nights when Lauren doesn't pass out from exhaustion, she reads almost every genre so, naturally, her writing reflects that. With every book and every story, you'll find elements of other genres—fantasy, mystery, romance, paranormal, suspense, YA, women's literature, all with a touch of humor.

Because what doesn't kill us should make us laugh.

**How to help your favorite authors
and make them eternally grateful**

Leave reviews
Tell your friends
Share their posts on social media
Recommend their books to readers' groups

www.ingramcontent.com/pod-product-compliance
Lightning Source LLC
Chambersburg PA
CBHW022203170626
46807CB00005B/2324